"Okay, we'r

Cleo's beautiful
husky laughter g
the gut. As she c
amusement fade
neck. "What are you thinking, Malcolm?"

"God, I want you. Why isn't it night? Why
did we think we needed kids? They're always
awake."

"Don't know." Her eyelids fluttered
downwards.

Dropping the hem of her sweatshirt, he turned
her around and boosted her up to his shoulder.
"You remember how to climb a tree, right?"

"Malcolm, what are you—" She looked down
at him, green eyes dancing. "In the tree
house?"

"You got a better idea? Go on, climb."

She lost her hold once because she was
giggling. "Aren't we too old for this?"

"God, I hope not."

Available in August 2006
from Silhouette Superromance

Hometown Girl
by Margaret Watson
(Suddenly a Parent)

The Chosen Child
by Brenda Mott
(Count on a Cop)

A Little Secret Between Friends
by CJ Carmichael

Coming Home
by Jean Brashear
(Mother & Child Reunion)

Coming Home
JEAN BRASHEAR

SILHOUETTE®
SuperROMANCE™

*Silhouette, Silhouette Superromance and Colophon are registered
trademarks of Harlequin Books S.A., used under licence.*

*First published in Great Britain 2006
Silhouette Books, Eton House, 18-24 Paradise Road,
Richmond, Surrey TW9 1SR*

© Jean Brashear 2005

*Standard ISBN 0 373 71251 0
Promotional ISBN 0 373 60492 0*

38-0806

*Printed and bound in Spain
by Litografia Rosés S.A., Barcelona*

Dear Reader,

Those familiar with my work understand how important family is to me and my belief that love can change the world. This MOTHER & CHILD REUNION series has haunted me as much as I have loved writing it. The power of love lost and found again strikes deep into this romantic's soul.

All Cleo Channing ever wanted was the stable home and big, loving family she never had as a child. When gorgeous and thoroughly normal Malcolm Channing swept her off her feet, she thought they had it all—beautiful children and a gracious old house she vowed to fill to the rafters with love.

But sometimes loving families still produce troubled children, and even the strongest bond can be tested beyond bearing. When unimaginable tragedy strikes Cleo's family, it is scattered to the winds. Years later the bad-seed child returns, still troubled but bearing an unexpected and precious gift. Cleo's and Malcolm's lives intersect once again, but formidable obstacles stand in the way of the love that never truly died.

The format of this series is unusual for series romance: the same flow of events mirrored in successive books but viewed through the eyes of opposing players. *Coming Home* is Cleo and Malcolm's story; in September their daughter Ria's side of the tale will be told in *Forgiveness*. I hope you'll be as touched by reading them as I was while writing them.

As always, I love hearing from readers, via my website (www.jeanbrashear.com) or www. eHarlequin.com. For postal mail: PO Box 3000 #79, Georgetown, TX 78627, USA.

All my best,

Jean Brashear

For beloved Emma, whose zest for life
enriches and charms us all.
May your dreams be as far-reaching as the
outdoors you so adore and may your life be
filled to the sky with love.

ACKNOWLEDGEMENTS

My heartfelt thanks to Laura Shin and Paula
Eykelhof for letting me spread my wings in
this amazing place called Superromance. I
have blossomed as a writer in this remarkable
world you have created, and I have never
been so challenged—or enjoyed it more.

I cannot say often enough how much I
appreciate my ever-amazing editor, Beverley
Sotolov, for so many acts of kindness and
support, and for her pivotal role in my growth.
I'm grateful that you saw the potential in this
mini-series concept—and even more so that
you never lost faith, no matter how often I
did. Thanks for being the voice of calm at the
other end of the crisis hotline!

CHAPTER ONE

Austin, Texas

GYPSY ROSE LEE danced in the backyard, performing a slow bump-and-grind for an old, half-blind dog. Tom Jones wailed the melody to a steady backbeat and more brass than the law should allow.

Cleo Channing could swear the squirrel sitting on a limb nearby was smiling.

Today Gypsy. Tomorrow Rita Hayworth, maybe a little Ava Gardner thrown in for good measure. As Cleo's seventy-four-year-old mother, Lola, danced, her brilliant purple-and-lime-green caftan flashed through pools of golden sunlight.

Cleo sighed. Snuggled into plump pillows on her private sunporch in the crisp autumn morning, she stared at the skyline of downtown Austin through the steam rising from her teacup. Tom Jones and Lola were playing havoc with her much-cherished indulgence, this tranquil time to gather herself before the day. She rose early to watch dawn kiss away the dew as cats prowled beneath the forsythia and birds greeted the sun. The steady hum of traffic from Lamar Boulevard below was background music, the pulse beat of a city coming to life.

She loved mornings, but she had missed a lot of them. Malcolm had always enjoyed sleeping until the last possible moment and had wanted her tucked in beside him.

But Malcolm had been gone for five years; he slept in a condo now, beside his younger woman. Who was welcome to him. Cleo had crawled her way to wholeness alone. She had her own life, and she liked it fine.

Or she'd been content with it before Lola and Aunt Cammie had shown up three months ago. Cammie was a sweetheart, but Lola had shattered the careful structure of Cleo's world. Once again, Cleo was forced to assume her childhood role as the adult in Lola's life; Aunt Cammie couldn't be expected to keep a lid on her sister's excesses. It boggled the mind to think that B-movie goddess Lola could have been born to the same parents as dainty, demure Camille.

But nothing could bother Cleo today. Not this day. And ironic as it was, Lola would probably approve of her plans.

Tonight, Cleo might very well take her first lover since the divorce.

She was more than nervous, yet a delicious shiver raced through her, and a part of her melted like dark chocolate under summer sun. She had fought the lure, telling herself she was too old and Colin too young, donning her iciest reserve…all for naught.

Fifty-one years old she was, and she should have no trouble thinking of Colin Spencer as a son. He was twelve years younger than she, for heaven's sake.

But he sang the praises of older women, teased her, calling her a puritan. Pursued her and refused to let her good sense discourage him.

Until she'd finally agreed to have dinner with him tonight—and not at the coffee shop he owned next door to her high-end gift store.

At his apartment. Where they both knew what might happen.

She had to be insane.

But, oh, she was tempted.

Where is your dignity, Cleo? It's not seemly, not seemly at all. The voices crowded in, as they did every day. In the past, she had succeeded in listening.

Until yesterday.

Now the former Mrs. Malcolm Channing,

mother, grandmother and respected business owner, was staring into the treetops—

And getting hot and bothered.

Her bedroom door opened a crack. Aunt Cammie peered around the edge, her expression apologetic. "I'm sorry. I knocked, but you didn't hear me."

Cleo blinked away her fantasies. "Difficult to hear anything over Tom Jones. What did you need?" Cammie moved through the house on silent cat feet, barely stirring the air, seldom speaking. She wouldn't have interrupted if it wasn't important.

Her distress registered on Cleo. "What's wrong?"

"I—" She glanced toward the door. "Would you please come downstairs?"

Cleo wanted to ask if it could wait until she'd soaked up her morning's peace. Or nestled in one more absurd fantasy of tonight.

Tom Jones wailed, and Cleo gave up. Serenity and Lola Fontaine lived in alternate universes. Only a faulty memory would allow Cleo to hope otherwise. She set down her cup, trailing one finger across its tiny painted violets, and rose, brushing aside the afghan as she slid her feet into satin slippers.

Aunt Cammie was already halfway down the stairs. Cleo barely noticed the smooth walnut beneath her hand as her mind jumped to possibilities. Her aunt was a former nurse who could handle a wide range of emergencies; she was gentle but always forthright. So what was going on?

Nearing the bottom of the stairs, Cleo noted the emotions leaping across Cammie's features. Unease. Compassion.

Yearning.

Even before Cleo turned in the same direction, something was already telling her that everything had changed.

"Hey," said the daughter Cleo hadn't seen in six years. The girl who'd made the ten years before that a living nightmare. Cleo couldn't quite register that Victoria was here, in the flesh. That she looked like hell.

But it was the sight of the little boy with her that sucked all the air out of the room.

"My God in heaven, he's the spitting image of David." Lola rushed past Cleo, caftan swirling around her tall figure.

Cleo hadn't even heard her mother come inside. She stood there frozen, hoping the pain couldn't pierce the calluses that bone-deep grief had built around her heart.

David. Her son, who'd been lost to them for six years. No one ever said his name anymore, as though he'd never existed. But he had. He did. Within Cleo's heart, the child who'd been an unexpected gift still lived. Still breathed.

Hadn't died at the hands of the wraith in her doorway.

Cleo tried to move her feet. Use her voice. Something to dance away from the boulder of longing rolling her way. Anything to keep from screaming at her firstborn.

"Mother—" Victoria's eyes, so empty and dark and hot, scraped at Cleo's heart…pleading for comfort and hope.

Cleo's conscience had almost pushed the message from brain to feet to propel her forward.

But not soon enough.

Gaunt and strained, Cleo's lost daughter shivered, a survivor close enough to safety to give up the struggle. The feverish glint left her eyes. With one shaking hand, she stroked the boy's hair.

Then, like a rag doll, Victoria crumpled to the floor.

CHAPTER TWO

"SHE'S ONLY FAINTED, honey. Your mother will be fine," Aunt Cammie said, glancing over at the child Cleo had removed to the kitchen to comfort.

"See?" Kneeling beside him, Cleo rubbed a slow circle on his back. "Aunt Cammie's a nurse, so you can take her word for it."

She couldn't even call him by his name, her own grandson. He looked too much like Victoria—dear God, like David—not to be a Channing. Yet they'd had no idea he existed.

Rage roared so loudly in her ears she could barely think. Knowing about him could have made such a difference to them all. Where had these two been? What had her daughter put him through?

The boy's bottom lip quivered. "Who are you?"

The carefully constructed casing around Cleo's heart cracked wide-open. She managed to still the rushing joy that made her want to crush him against her, to fight everyone to protect him. Clearing a throat gone suddenly tight, she touched his cheek.

"I'm your mama's mama."

Baby soft. Human silk. She let her fingers trail over his hair and realized how badly he needed a bath.

Victoria, what have you done?

With effort, she steadied her voice. "I have two granddaughters who call me Nana, but you can choose whatever you'd like. Would you tell me your name, sweetheart?"

His gaze was uncertain as he shrugged. "It's Benjy."

"That's a very fine name. Is it short for Benjamin?"

Benjy studied her with Malcolm's brown eyes beneath a shaggy fringe of her own black hair. "Benjamin David," he corrected.

Benjamin…*David*. A shudder rippled down her spine. Cut off her breath.

Oh, God. Malcolm. She would have to call him. He would be as shocked as she was. And maybe as aware of the passage of time. Of the love that hadn't been able to survive the pain.

She yanked her thoughts back to the boy. The present. "Are you hungry, Benjy?"

A solemn nod. "Can my mom eat, too?"

"Of course, but right now she's really tired. Are you?" She studied him. He needed a bath and clean clothes, but at least Victoria's son didn't have the pinched look of starvation that rode his mother's frame.

"I hate naps."

Cleo laughed, and a shy smile peeked out from his dark eyes. "So did—" *David*. Oh, this was hard, so hard. "I bet we could make some French toast. Does that sound good?"

"I never had French toast. Is it like regular toast?"

She bit her lip, then brightened her voice. "Even better. You can have cinnamon and powdered sugar or syrup on it. Do you want milk to drink, or would you prefer orange juice?"

"I like milk." He regarded her warily. "Do you have enough?"

Tears pricked at Cleo's eyes that he would worry. She gathered him into her arms and pressed him to her heart as she'd been dying to do since the front door opened. "Sweetheart, we have plenty. And we can get more. You drink all the milk you can hold."

To her great relief, he didn't seem to mind the hug. Small hands slid around her back while he leaned into her body. Cleo closed her eyes and soaked up the feel of him. *Malcolm, you're going to love him so.*

Then, as lightning heralds a storm, she felt the atmosphere crackle even before she heard the voice.

"Benjy, what's wrong?"

Victoria.

"Mom!" The boy wriggled out of Cleo's arms and raced to his mother. "Are you okay? I was scared."

"I'm just fine, sweetie."

Cleo faced her daughter slowly, fighting back fury. Fear. "Victoria…" She proceeded with caution. "Should you be up?"

"My name is Ria."

Ri— How could she? That had been David's special name for her.

The green eyes so like Cleo's own were fierce and raw. Her daughter clutched Benjy to her side, one hand spread protectively across the back of his head. The warning was clear. Nothing had changed between Cleo and her lost daughter.

"Why—" Cleo battled for composure. "What brought you here, Victo—Ria? Is something—" *Wrong?* Bitter laughter bubbled up in her throat. Of course it was. Nothing had been right with her for years.

Anger flared in her daughter's gaze, but beneath it, Cleo thought she saw a flash of sorrow. "Never mind. We're out of here. Benjy—"

"No—" Cleo grabbed her daughter's arm. "Don't—"

Victoria stiffened. "Let go of me."

She was so thin. So…fragile. Cleo forced herself to remove her hand. "Please. Don't…leave."

A fine trembling seized her daughter's frame.

"Don't hurt my mom." Benjy's voice quivered.

"Oh, sweetheart, I'd never—" But she had. She
and her eldest had wounded each other time and
time again. "I didn't mean—I want you both to
stay, that's all."

His eyes filled with confusion.

"Your mother might need to see a doctor, sweetheart. I'd like to take you both, only to be sure—"

"Afraid we've got fleas, Mother?" Color rose
in her daughter's face. "Just because we've been
living in my car doesn't mean we have cooties or
carry a dread disease. A bath will suffice." Her
voice went sharper. "I'll clean your pristine tub
afterward."

"Please don't, Vic—Ria. Not in front of—"
Cleo compressed her lips and gestured toward
Benjy. "I was about to make Benjy French toast.
Perhaps you'd care for some, too?"

A bark of laughter, harsh and ugly. "Nothing
gets through the Teflon, does it, Mother? Always
the perfect hostess."

Caustic words leaped to Cleo's tongue, but she
saw Benjy's face. He darted glances between his
mother and Cleo.

"Whatever you think of me, consider your child,

at least. Let him eat his breakfast in peace." Salty tears raked the back of her eyes. Cleo blinked hard before they could fall. "Aunt Cammie, would you mind—" She looked around in a desperate attempt to find her balance. "I—if you'll excuse me, I must open the shop."

The last thing she wanted was to go to work today, but her younger daughter, Betsey, had to be at her daughters' preschool, and the new clerk couldn't handle things by herself yet. And her handyman, Sandor, was due to install new cabinets similar to those he'd built for Colin.

Colin. Oh, no. She'd been out of her mind; she saw that now. Tonight's plans were out of the question.

With quick steps, she headed for the doorway, giving her daughter wide berth.

"Where's Daddy?" Victoria's words froze Cleo in her tracks.

Cleo and Lola exchanged glances.

"He doesn't live here anymore." She inhaled, braced for the assault. "We're divorced."

"What?" Victoria blinked, then narrowed her eyes. "Congratulations. You drove him away, too."

Each word clawed at tender, unhealed flesh. *Did I?* Cleo wondered. *Or did he let me down when I needed him most?* But she held her tongue, watching the boy whose plight tore at her heart.

With a hand she wished weren't shaking, she brushed his hair once more.

She lifted her gaze to her daughter's, longing for some magic to make things different between them. With this child of hers, words were sticks of dynamite, all with lit fuses, some shorter than others. She had never been sure which ones would explode in her hand.

She didn't bother defending herself. "I'll let Malcolm know you're here." Holding herself erect, she exited the room. Aunt Cammie would take care of the basics.

Time had done nothing to change things between her and Victoria, but there was an innocent child to protect. The best thing she could do for the boy, staring at both of them with wide, frightened eyes, was to leave.

CHAPTER THREE

MALCOLM CHANNING WOKE when the toilet flushed. Sleepily, he reached across chilled sheets for Vanessa, then squinted toward the clock and frowned. He had ten minutes yet.

Damn. He'd been dreaming of David, of shooting hoops with his only son, and he wanted to go back. The glow of pleasure tightened into a fast, hard knot of sorrow.

Grief was like that—you'd go along for months, even years, thinking it was done with you. You'd be sure that, at last, you'd found your footing, that the worst was over. That although nothing would ever be the same again, you'd somehow managed to adapt to the new normal and things were under control. He had a setup many would admire: a solid balance sheet, high-end condo in exclusive Westlake Hills, a smart, beautiful, successful woman his friends envied him for.

Then something small and unexpected would

streak into his field of vision and with no warning would rip away the scab of six years' making.

It didn't happen often now, thank God. But for one crazy, impulsive second, still caught in the snare of the dream, Malcolm wanted to call Cleo. To talk about their boy, to make him real again, to hold him here.

But he and Cleo never spoke anymore. She had her life; he had his. Twenty-eight years of marriage had vanished like smoke in the ashes of David's death and Victoria's disappearance. They had hung on for a year of agony, long months when their every word had been tainted with pain. Finally, she'd begged him to leave for a while. Equally stunned by the plea as desperate for a solution, he'd complied. Cleo had watched him go with relief in her eyes. They'd no longer been able to see anything but grief and blame when they looked at each other.

He'd never intended the separation to become permanent, but soon divorce papers had arrived. Like a man betrayed and captured behind the lines of battle, wounded and shell-shocked, he'd signed them. What little he knew of Cleo's life now came in fragments dropped by their daughter Betsey. Cleo had opened her West Sixth Street gift shop after their divorce and made a success of it. He passed by every day on his way home from work, and some days, he wondered what would happen if he stopped.

He never did. There was no point. Cleo had made the transition, and so had he. He had Vanessa now. Did Cleo have someone? He couldn't quite hope she did.

The shower began, and Malcolm slid out of bed, then padded across the pale carpet. On his way, he glanced in the mirror over the bureau. Not bad. At fifty-five, he could probably pass for mid-forties. He biked; he worked out five days a week; he took the stairs instead of the elevator; he watched what he ate.

When you had a woman in your life who was twenty years younger, you'd better damn well watch your waistline. He didn't kid himself that Vanessa would stick around if he didn't. He thought she cared about him, but Malcolm didn't assume that she would be there when he was old. He'd never asked her to marry him, likely never would. She hadn't mentioned it, either.

Vanessa was into success and ambition. She'd carved out an impressive career as a lobbyist, and she rubbed shoulders with power every day. Sleek and blond and tall, she had a softer side, but it seldom showed. He didn't doubt she would regret losing the good times if they parted, but she was not the nurturing sort. Malcolm was a well-connected and successful investor, but if he lost his edge, she'd be gone, and Malcolm knew it. It was what he had liked about her from the beginning— that she would never break his heart.

Because he would never love her. Love could heal, but it could devastate. He'd save what was left of the emotion that had once pervaded his every cell for his daughter Betsey's two girls. For Betsey, who tried so hard to be enough now that her siblings were gone.

When he shoved open the bathroom door, Vanessa backed away from the mirror and stepped quickly into the shower without a word of greeting. Malcolm frowned. It wasn't often that they showered together, but that wouldn't account for the look on her face, one he'd seen several times recently. Almost anger—but he could think of nothing he'd done to provoke it.

He opened the glass door and entered. "Are you all right?"

With jerky motions, she lathered the shampoo into high peaks and nodded, still facing away from him.

Malcolm stroked her back, leaning down to nip at her shoulder. Vanessa stiffened. He placed his hands on her hips and slowly turned her toward him. "What is it?"

Pale. A bit guilty. "Nothing. I have to be in the office early."

He took her chin in his hand and studied eyes that flared in defiance. "How early?" But the smile that usually drew one from her—the one she claimed to adore—wasn't working.

"Too soon." She turned and rinsed, but not before he saw something like apology in her expression.

Malcolm took the conditioner out of her hands and poured some in one palm. Then he proceeded to massage it into her scalp and smooth it through her golden hair. Normally she would relax. Sometimes, it even constituted foreplay.

Not today. Shoulders rigid, she waited as though a racehorse ready to run, a nearly imperceptible trembling in her frame. The second he finished, she moved under the shower flow.

"What is it, hon? Don't try to tell me there's nothing wrong."

She whirled, and her feet slipped from beneath her. Malcolm caught her against him, and for one moment she relaxed, leaning her forehead against his jaw, her breath warm against his skin.

"I—" She shook her head. "No, Malcolm." Straightening, she grabbed the door handle and pushed. "Not right now."

If her voice hadn't quivered, he would have let her go. Vanessa was not an easy woman to live with, subject to mood swings, solitary by nature, driven and focused and seldom relaxed. But this was something different. Somehow, she appeared…vulnerable.

Vulnerable? Vanessa?

Malcolm cut off the shower and stepped out. He would finish later.

"What is it, babe?"

"Don't call me babe. It's demeaning." She cranked up the blow-dryer, making it impossible to talk.

Malcolm ignored the retort and considered her while he wrapped a towel around his waist. Long, smooth flanks, small, high breasts, hips that barely flared from a slender waist. A thoroughbred down to her toes, she wore clothes like a mannequin, a perfect size six and only a few inches shorter than his own six foot two.

Vanessa glanced at him in the mirror and shut off the dryer, then donned the robe she rarely wore. Tying it tightly around her waist, she moved toward her closet.

Malcolm grabbed her arm. "Vanessa, something's wrong, and I want to know what. Is it work?"

She jerked away and kept going. "No."

"Anything I did?"

She snorted, but the sound was elegant, as was everything about Vanessa.

"How the hell am I supposed to fix it if I have no idea what it is?"

"I didn't ask you to fix it." She pondered her clothes as though the meaning of life lay draped over a hanger.

"Fine." Malcolm stalked out of the room and wondered why he didn't live alone. Cleo had done so since the divorce and from all reports was doing fine.

But he understood why. He liked waking up with a woman, enjoyed sleeping with one tucked against him. Relished the way they smelled and the mess they made of his bathroom with all their bottles and potions. This place was too antiseptic after all the years of kids and pets and bikes on the lawn. He'd thought that not being surrounded by clutter, in something new and bright that required no mowing or paint-ing, would be a welcome relief. But every day, it mocked him.

He could live alone all right. Maybe he would again soon. If he required any assurance that he didn't love Vanessa, the lack of pain in that thought should have told him for certain.

Feeling a little guilt at the ease with which he could let her go, Malcolm turned back toward the bathroom and pushed open the door.

Vanessa stood in her closet, her face in her hands and shoulders shaking.

If the sun had come up in the west that day, Malcolm couldn't have been more shocked. Vanessa didn't cry—ever. He'd never been certain her tear ducts functioned.

Malcolm crossed the expanse of tile and glass, came up behind her and placed his hands on her shoulders. Vanessa recoiled, wiping at her cheeks with the palms of her hands.

"Whatever it is, I'll help you, Vanessa. Just talk to me."

"Damn you, I'm pregnant."

Shock sizzled down his spine, followed by a joy so intense he could barely speak. Malcolm forgot that he didn't love her, that two minutes before, he'd been ready to let her go.

A child. *His* child.

"But that's great, honey!" He smiled with the rush of a pleasure so visceral he shivered.

"I'm not having it." Her chin jutted, her eyes sparking with mutiny.

"What? Why?"

"I don't want children, Malcolm. I have no idea how this happened. I was so careful. It ruins everything." Always-elegant Vanessa all but wailed out her accusation.

"No need to be hasty. Take some time to get used to the idea. We can get married right away. We can—" He started pacing the room. "I'll find out about a license today, and John will marry us—" He turned back and studied her belly for signs of rounding. "When is it due?"

Her eyes turned to stone. "I don't want to get married."

"Okay, you prefer to be nonconformist about this. It leads to so many questions later, when a child is older, and it's not really fair to the child, but we can talk—"

"You're not listening to me, Malcolm." The voice snapped each word out like gunfire. "I—do—not—want—this—baby."

Malcolm could not believe how much the words hurt him. Or that five minutes ago, he'd been prepared to live a different life. Now everything was changed. His baby was stirring to life in this woman's body.

Still he tried to be objective. "Because it's mine?"

The eyes softened then. Vanessa shook her head. "No, that's not it. If I—" Her voice caught. "If I were going to have a child, you'd be a perfect father."

He smiled in relief. "You're just nervous. Hey, I've got lots of experience with kids. I'll show you the ropes."

Her tone hardened again. "I know you would. But it doesn't change anything. I don't want to be a mother, Malcolm. I never did." She moved away. "I'll make an appointment to handle it. I hadn't planned to tell you, and I'm sorry I slipped."

Rage all but blinded him. He jerked her around. "You can't get rid of my child. I won't let you."

"What are you going to do? Tie me to a chair until it's born?"

He could see that she meant it. If she was bent on proceeding, there was nothing to prevent her.

Malcolm eased his grip on her elbow and dragged a deep breath into his lungs. Where was his leverage? Suddenly, this child's life was everything. He had to find a way to stop her. "I'm sorry. I don't— Vanessa, I'll beg if I must. Please don't do this."

"I can't be a mother, Malcolm. Don't ask me to. I just can't." Fear leaped high in her eyes.

"You only think that because this is new to you. You'll handle it as well as you do everything else. And I really am good at parenthood. I'll teach you."

Her voice lowered in sympathy. "This is about David, isn't it?"

"Of course not." Instantly, he was sorry he'd ever shared any of his pain. Her expression made it clear that she pitied him, and he understood then that he had no desire to raise a child with this woman, didn't want her as his baby's mother. She was nothing like—

Cleo. Damn. Why couldn't it be Cleo here right now? She would rejoice with him. She would be thrilled, already mentally redecorating a room for a nursery. But Cleo's baby-making days were over. He'd thought his were, too. To care about this so much was insane, but he did. Whatever was required, this child must survive.

"Okay. You don't have to marry me. You can walk away, scot-free, once it's born. Name your price, Vanessa."

Her eyes went wide. "You can't raise a child alone."

"The hell I can't."

"Malcolm, you're too—" She halted, but he understood what she meant.

"I'm not too old, and I'm in great health. Men in my family live a long time. I'd have the money to retire right now if I decided to do it. I can afford help."

"Maybe it's not your child."

She was lying, but the thought stopped him cold. Why did this mean so much? Was he grasping for a shield against aging? A second chance? Another bid for immortality because his name would go on?

Malcolm had no idea and didn't wish to think about any of that now. He had to buy time. "You may not want to raise it, but do you really have it in you to do this, Vanessa?"

Her chin thrust forward. "It's my choice to make."

"Is it?" he challenged.

The tension ratcheted. The room went silent, the air around them charged.

Her words sent panic slamming through his veins. He'd have defended any woman's right to make the choice—until this moment. But now it wasn't simply an idea, some abstract debate. This was his baby, and he couldn't be philosophical anymore.

As anger rose, he caught a look at her face. She wasn't just mad. She was scared.

Slow down, he told himself. *You're going at her too fast, too hard.*

And to be fair, the pregnancy affected her more. He could be responsible for everything once that child was born, but he couldn't handle the next several months for her. Couldn't prevent the thoroughbred frame from changing.

"I'm sorry. It was wrong of me to say that." Suddenly, he lacked the words. At the most critical juncture of his life, his glib tongue failed him. All he had left was his heart.

"This has to be a shock for you. I understand how important your career is and that this doesn't fit into any of your plans."

He raked tense fingers through his hair and began to pace. "Maybe you're right. This might be about David more than I want to admit. And yes, I'm not young anymore, but I'm a long way from the grave. Plenty of men have become fathers at my age."

Malcolm faced her. "You've never held your child in your arms, but I have. There's nothing that even comes close." He felt a spark of hope from the indecision flickering across her features and took his first deep breath since she'd confessed. "You might like it, Van, more than you realize."

She stiffened again. "I doubt that."

He tamped down his anger. There would be no second chance if he blew it now. "Fine. Maybe you're right. But the fact remains that it's my child, too."

He could see her protest forming and held up one hand to stop it. "All I'm asking for is time for both of us to think."

"I don't have much left."

"I'm sorry." And he was. This had to be wreaking havoc inside her. Watching for signs that she would shy away again, he reached for her. She remained stiff. "Please, Vanessa. Just promise you won't take any actions without talking to me first. The legislature's not in session this next year, so your workload will be lighter. I could spirit you off somewhere so that no one would know. You've labored hard for a long time—you've earned a sabbatical. Who's to complain if your lover decides to pamper you?"

"I could lose all my contacts, Malcolm. Six months is too long to be gone."

"You've got a solid reputation. There's e-mail. Phones, faxes. You can stay in touch. Please, Van. Just give me a chance to figure out a solution."

She stared at him silently.

Malcolm held his breath.

"You've got one week."

"A month. Give me a month. My business doesn't wrap up easily."

"Neither does mine."

Of course she was right. But this was too important. If he had to, he'd cancel every contract he had going. "Two weeks."

Vanessa stared at him. "Two weeks. But don't get your hopes up."

He held out a hand to signal agreement on the most critical negotiation of his life. Summoned a smile to hide the nerves. "I'll make you an offer you can't turn down."

Her slender hand clasped his larger one. "Your charm won't be enough, Malcolm, potent though it is. I do business with charming men every day."

He was certain then that their relationship was over, regardless. Whatever had brought them together, Malcolm looked at Vanessa Wainwright and realized that he'd been drifting from day to day, week to week, piling up money too easily while puffing his chest that a beautiful, much-younger woman was on his arm and in his bed.

He'd once had a life that had cut to the marrow of existence. He'd poured his heart into his children; he'd loved a woman down to his soul—

He'd lost all of it. Walked away stunned like a survivor of a bomb blast, living only in the moment and forgetting what was truly important.

There was nothing Malcolm could do to bring David back. To reclaim the lost daughter he feared he'd never see again. And Cleo? She'd gone on without him. All that had been good in his life was over.

But inside the belly of a woman who didn't want it lay his chance for redemption.

Negotiation was his lifeblood, structuring compromises and win-win situations. He would find a way with this, the most important deal he'd ever attempted.

CLEO SLOWED as she approached the back door of her shop. The door was half-open in deference to the crisp, cool air, which meant that Sandor was inside, busy as usual.

Sandor Miklós Wolfe had entered her life as an act of mercy, but he had become her cherished friend. Raised in Hungary by his grandmother, he had arrived in Austin nearly a year ago at the age of thirty-four to experience the world of the American father, long dead, whom he had never met.

He was the hardest worker she'd ever known. He'd come to the shop seeking employment she couldn't afford to offer, but he had quickly shown her, through a series of odd jobs that desperately needed doing, that it would be folly to refuse him. He had worked too cheap, and when she'd discovered that he had no place to stay, she'd allowed him to set up a cot in her storeroom.

Along the way, she'd stumbled upon his true gift, practiced late at night, for wood carving. She constantly urged him to let her show his work to gallery owners she knew, but thus far, he'd refused, calling it only a hobby.

In the meantime, he sought out jobs from others and saved nearly every cent, paying cash for his tools and an old pickup and, a few days ago, making a deal to trade repairs for rent on a garage apartment not far away.

He still did his carving in her storeroom, but she would lose that soon, she imagined. His daily presence was so comforting that she wasn't eager for him to leave.

Today, she could use a friend to help her sort through the turmoil. Sandor was the best listener she'd ever met. She picked up her pace across the grassy, tree-shaded expanse, needing to get a grip on herself before she phoned Malcolm.

At that moment, however, Colin stepped out of

the back door of his coffee shop, white pastry box in hand.

Normally, she would have experienced a small thrill, part joy, part anticipation, laced less and less with self-consciousness. When she'd awakened this morning, she had felt much more.

But this day was not normal, nor was it the one it had been just a few hours ago. Her calm, orderly new life, already strained by three months of Lola, was ready to burst at the seams. The small steps she'd danced closer to Colin's lure were giant leaps toward being a fool.

Who was she kidding? She was firmly middle-aged, teetering on the edge of indignity. And now there were eyes to watch her do it. Her pretty new brass bed, which she'd bought to replace the wooden one Malcolm had made for her, would remain chaste.

"Good morning." His expression brightened at the sight of her. He stopped only a breath away.

For a moment, Cleo couldn't find her voice, so sharp was her longing. He had barely ever touched her except a hand to an elbow, a palm to her back, but in her mind his hands had been...everywhere. In the heart of the night, she had buried imaginary fingers in that unruly black hair, had pressed wish-filled lips to the mobile mouth. Had treasured once more the welcome weight of a man's body covering her own.

His smile dimmed. "What's wrong, Cleo?"

His eyes were tender, eager. Heated. Cleo mourned the loss of something she'd wanted, ridiculous or not. Anger rode to her rescue.

She straightened. "Nothing. Only some unexpected company." Briskly, she continued. "I'm sorry, but I'll have to cancel our dinner, Colin."

He frowned but nodded. "We can reschedule. How long will your company be here?"

Cleo couldn't meet his eyes. Couldn't carry this off if she did. "I don't know."

A long pause. Then a chuckle. "I got it. You've lost your nerve again, haven't you?"

"Don't mock me, Colin." The anger she'd been suppressing all morning bumped at the lid she'd slammed on it. "I was foolish to think— You could be my son," she accused.

His sigh was eloquent. "How often do we have to confront this, Cleo? You were just a kid when I was born, but the point is moot. We're not kids now. There's no law against good, healthy sex between people who enjoy each other. I care about you, Cleo. I admire you. There's no reason to be so afraid."

"I'm not." Though he was wrong; there were plenty of reasons. And too much atumble inside her this morning. "I don't want to talk about it."

He grabbed her arm. "You never do. Listen,

it doesn't have to be a big deal. Why can't you see that?"

But it was a big deal. She'd only made love with one man in her life. She yanked from his grasp and drew herself up, wishing she were taller. "We have nothing in common, Colin. The idea was ridiculous. I don't know why I ever—" She reversed course and stumbled.

"Whoa, careful." Colin clutched at her.

Embarrassed nearly to the point of tears she'd rather die than shed, she slapped at his hand. "Don't." She hated the shrillness of her voice.

"I was only trying—"

"Just—get out of here—"

"Is something wrong, Cleopatra?" A low baritone behind her.

Sandor. Thank God.

"I—no, it's—"

"Are you certain?" Tall and blond and unsmiling, he was beside her then, towering over Colin.

Colin stared at her. "Cleo, I'd never hurt you."

"Perhaps you could return later, Colin." Sandor's tone made clear that it wasn't a suggestion.

Colin's head snapped up, and he glared at Sandor. "Yeah, sure. Here—" He shoved the pastry box into Sandor's hands. His shoulders sagged. "I don't understand."

"Me, either." She sniffed and wiped beneath

her eyes. "It's not your fault, Colin. I just—things—" She turned her palms upward. "I'm sorry."

Colin took a step toward her. From the corner of her eye, she saw Sandor shake his head.

Colin halted. Seemed unbearably young. Finally, he threw up his palms. "Have a good day."

And he was gone, striding off with hurt and confusion riding on his shoulders.

She buried her face in her hands. "He's a good man. He deserves better."

"As do you. Shh…" Sandor clasped her elbow, led her into the shop and closed the door behind them. He settled her on the sofa in her office, then placed the pastry box on the desk and crouched before her. "What has happened, Cleo?"

"Nothing's—" She abandoned pretense. "My daughter arrived on my doorstep this morning."

"Betsey is well?"

"Not Betsey. Victoria—Ria, as she wants to be called."

"What does she want?"

"I don't know. Shelter, perhaps. Probably money, as well." She shot him a glance. "She has a little boy. They were both filthy and hungry. They've been living in her car for God knows how long."

Then she studied the ground, her voice barely a whisper. "He looks like David."

Sandor knew the story, told one night when they were both working late after the shop had closed. "I see. So you will take him in and feed him because he is your flesh. You will care for him both for himself and for the son you can no longer hold."

Cleo nodded.

"And Victoria? What will you do with her?"

"She hates me still. There's so much anger in her."

"But if you send her away, you will lose the boy."

"Yes." Despair settled over her like wet wool.

Sandor shook his head. "So much to fret over, even for you, the Madonna of Perpetual Worry."

"And now I have to call Malcolm."

"How will he react?"

"He'll probably side with her, as always." She sighed. "I have no desire to fight with her anymore. I only—" She struggled against hopelessness. "I wish for my family back," she whispered. "The way it used to be."

Hot tears scalded the back of her throat. "I was sure I'd put it behind me, but seeing her today, knowing that she hasn't changed—" Cleo sat up very straight. "She has no right to that boy. She can't be trusted."

Suddenly, Cleo had a goal that would lead her out of the quicksand that had sucked at her ankles since Victoria had walked through the door. "I'm going to ensure that Benjy has the life he deserves. I will not stand by and let her harm another child."

Sandor's eyes did not grant her the approval she'd expected. "You have little information about their relationship."

She tilted her chin. "I know more than she does about being a mother."

"But you are not his."

Fury renewed her strength. "You have no children, Sandor. You can't possibly understand."

"This boy is not David. Saving him will not give you back your son."

Didn't he think she was all too aware of that?

An uncomfortable silence loomed.

Eventually, Sandor broke it. "So what happened with Colin this morning?"

"Nothing." Not true, but she was too embarrassed at her lapse of control to discuss it.

"You are breaking his heart, Cleopatra."

She gasped. "I have no idea what you mean."

When she rose abruptly and began fussing with the teapot, he chuckled. "Oh, my friend, you are so American sometimes. If that is your best impression of an elderly spinster, I am afraid you need more practice."

"Sandor, it's not what you—I mean, we aren't—"

"You think the attraction between you is invisible?

Do not tell me—you have rejected him with some sort of argument about your remarkably advanced age."

She set the teapot down with a barely restrained thud. "I don't want to discuss this. It's—I'm… ridiculous." She quickened her steps and made to enter the showroom.

"Cleo, stop. I apologize. I can see this pains you, and that is the last thing I want."

She stood with her back to him, struggling to find solid ground.

"Talk to me, my friend. Tell me what has happened to make you feel old again."

He'd put his finger on the problem, as always. Slowly, she faced him. Sandor's eyes were like his soul—older than his body and much too perceptive.

"It's just—" How did she explain that Colin had made her see herself as desirable and beautiful in a way she'd thought never to experience again? Without ever even kissing her, he had pressed at the seams of her armor, sliding it away from her one plate at a time, and had transformed the dried-up woman she was in danger of becoming.

Colin's interest had made her feel juicy again, ripe and succulent like a fruit ready to drop, an apple turned a perfect red on the tree. Even when Lola had fallen on hard times and Cleo had made the decision to take her and Aunt Cammie in, she'd kept Colin her delicious secret. She was still the youngest in a house full of women, the one who might have possibilities and potential. Lola was too self-absorbed to notice, and Aunt Cammie would never chide her, even if she was aware.

But Victoria's arrival, child in tow, had reminded Cleo that she was the mother of someone who would view Cleo's attraction to Colin as foolish. Ridiculous, even.

"I am too old for him. It's a simple fact."

"He is an adult, Cleo. He knows his mind. And you are a beautiful woman, one who has been solitary for too long. Why can you not allow yourself a little pleasure? Who will it harm?"

"I can't discuss this with you, Sandor. It's not… proper." Nor was following through with Colin.

"And with whom can you?"

Who indeed? Once there had been Malcolm, who had plumbed the secrets of her soul; since then…no one. The road to accepting her solitude had been a long one, but Cleo should be accustomed to dealing with life on her own by now. "There's nothing to talk over. I've come to my senses."

"Cleo…" Sandor's dismay was evident. "Very well. I will drop it for now, but I will not cease to remind you that you are far from dead and deserve more than you allow yourself." He walked to the back door, then paused. "Please remember that above all I am your friend. I will be here, should you change your mind."

The tears she'd been fighting all morning nearly got the best of her. "Thank you, Sandor. You're very kind to me."

He shook his head sadly. "If only you would follow my example." He left.

She watched him go, then with a long sigh made her way to unlock the front door. She was tired already, and she still had to call the man she hadn't talked to in forever and break the news that the daughter who had cost them everything...was back.

CHAPTER FOUR

San Francisco,
1971

SEVENTEEN-YEAR-OLD Cleo hurried down Fulton Street after work. Her mother was gone for the weekend, off with yet another yacht-club member who was sure to pave their way down easy street. Cleo was the one who squirreled away the rent money before Lola could spend it; Lola kept them on the move in pursuit of a dream.

Pulling up her collar against the stiff breeze, Cleo ignored how cold her feet were, concentrating instead on her list. A whole weekend by herself. Homework first, of course, and a head start on that term paper for history. She had her life mapped out, and college was the next step.

But for two glorious days, she'd have blessed quiet. Leisure to take a bubble bath. To read without interruption. Maybe even a chance to re-cover the old rocking chair she'd rescued from the alley.

She was so lost in anticipation that she didn't see the stranger until she ran into a wall of chest.

She recoiled. Lost her balance.

Strong hands steadied her. "Whoa, what's happenin', pretty girl?"

The voice had a drawl. The tone was friendly. But Haight-Ashbury had been taken over by hippies, and Cleo had a brush-off ready before she ever lifted her head.

And looked into the warmest pair of brown eyes she'd ever seen.

"You all right?"

"Yes. Fine." She shifted to walk around him.

"Sorry, miss. I wasn't watching where I was going."

Miss. Cleo lifted her head to discern whether he was mocking her. Then she noticed that he wasn't wearing a coat; that his jeans, though worn, were pressed with a crease. That his ancient work boots appeared almost spit-shined.

"That's okay. Now, if you'll excuse me—"

"Oh—sure. I just wondered—"

Here it came, the request for the handout. She tightened her grip on her purse and glanced around to check for help nearby, should he take her refusal poorly. "I'm sorry. I don't believe in handouts."

He recoiled. "You think I want—" His face flushed bright with insult. "No way."

"Then what do you—" She caught a good look at his eyes just then and realized that he was lonely. "You're a long way from home, aren't you?"

He frowned, still incensed, then exhaled. Grinned. "What gave me away—the accent or the lack of a coat?" He shivered slightly, and the breeze ruffled his thick, mink-brown hair.

"San Francisco is very cold in June."

"You're telling me. I thought California was supposed to be the land of surf and sun. You mind if we duck back out of the breeze? I'm supposed to pretend I'm not chilled to the bone, being a strong manly sort and all, but…"

Cleo couldn't stifle a laugh.

The brown eyes twinkled back.

He was a few years older, she thought. Tall. Charming. Cleo knew better than to trust that, though. Lola's men were often charming.

But Lola's men were smooth and slick. This one was different. Not polished at all, natural, even a little raw around the edges…and oddly appealing.

He shivered again.

She glanced up at the storefront sign and made a snap decision. "Want to get a cup of coffee?" Then she realized he might be down on his luck. "My treat?"

His brows drew together. "I'm from the old school, miss. I'm afraid you'll have to let me buy."

He pulled one hand out of his pocket for a shake. "I'm Malcolm Channing. Wouldn't do for you to go inside with a stranger, you know."

That smile again, irresistible in the lean, handsome face.

Cleo gave him her hand, still gloved. "Cleo Formby. I'm pleased to meet you, Mr. Channing."

He winced. "You seem pretty young, but come on, *Mr.* Channing?"

She couldn't help grinning. "You're the one calling me *miss.* And a gentleman isn't supposed to ask a lady's age."

Eyes glowing with mischief, he leaned down from his six-foot-plus height to whisper, "My mama would kick my tail from here to Waco if she heard that I had. You won't tell on me, will you?"

Cleo surprised herself by teasing back. "Is Waco far?"

"Darlin', it's a long way from anywhere." He gestured for her to precede him. "So is Cleo short for Cleopatra?"

"Those are fighting words, buddy."

He rubbed his hands together. "Oh, good. I haven't seen any of my brothers for weeks now. I'm spoiling for a fight."

The hostess ushered them to a booth. Malcolm helped Cleo out of her coat, and she nearly swooned at his manners.

"Brothers? How many?"

"Three. And two sisters."

She resisted a sigh. "How wonderful to have such a big family. Where are you from?"

"Texas. You?"

"Native Californian."

"You look like some hothouse flower from back East."

"Not all California girls are tall and blond and wear bikinis." She'd spent years praying for a growth spurt.

He shrugged. "I'm thinking my type might have to change to china dolls with black hair and green eyes."

The come-on had Cleo drawing back against the vinyl. She'd never learned how to flirt.

He leaned forward, eyes widening. "I just realized who you remind me of. Snow White in the storybook my mama read to us."

Cleo's tone went as rigid as her spine. Maybe he wasn't any different after all. "I'm not a character in a fairy tale, Malcolm—or some china doll."

"You don't like that." He lifted a shoulder. "Fine. Maybe you're not, but somebody ought to be pampering you." Then he leaned back and stretched out his arms across the back of the booth. "How old are you, anyway? You got a big brother who's gonna come whip my tail for making time with his pretty little sister?" He winked, his smile sure and easy. This was no boy, strutting and posturing like the ones she knew at school. This was a man, comfortable inside his skin.

"Just me and my mother." Maybe she should leave, but she didn't want to. "I'm almost eighteen, and if you ever call me Cleopatra, I'll kill you."

Malcolm laughed loudly, drawing the attention of the other diners. He nodded for the waitress to come take their coffee orders and somehow managed to talk Cleo into having dinner.

She watched how the waitress stared at Malcolm and noticed that more than one woman in the place cast second and third glances his way. When he got up to go to the rest room, female eyes followed him, smiles winged in his direction. He didn't seem to register any of them. Instead, he focused on her, and the effect was narcotic. She'd never met anyone like him.

Two hours passed in a blur. They had dessert, then endless cups of coffee, talking about everything imaginable. She learned that he was twenty-one and from Austin, Texas, that he was here out of curiosity, that he'd worked his way across the country on his summer break from college, living in his van so he could save money for his last year and still check out the crazy hippies in California.

His tastes in reading were eclectic, as were

hers—everything from Hermann Hesse to Louis L'Amour. He loved his big family, had played three sports in high school, and was pretty sure he was going to break his father's heart when he didn't go to law school after graduation.

He was this big, utterly normal American male, a creature so exotic to Cleo's experience that she was fairly certain no force on earth could make her forget him.

That very insight yanked her to her feet. "It's getting dark. We still have to find your van."

Malcolm's head cocked as he studied her. "All right." He helped her into her coat.

As they walked, he took her hand. His own, big and callused, swallowed hers up. Cleo had a sense of safety she'd never experienced before.

But he was a stranger and would soon be heading back to Texas. She was shocked at the depth of her regret over that. When he insisted on driving her home, she didn't refuse. Once there, though, she forced herself to alight from his van with a quick, cool thanks.

She didn't expect Malcolm to follow.

On the sidewalk, silence fell between them for the first time all night.

She'd become so comfortable with him that it felt as if they'd met each other years ago, not hours. Anyway, through all the moves with Lola,

Cleo had had to become a good judge of character.

Still, her next words amazed her. "Would you like to come in?"

His eyes widened in surprise. "You shouldn't be asking that of a man you just met."

She was both flustered and furious. "Who put you in charge?"

"Let me ask you this, then." One eyebrow lifted. "Is your mother home?"

"No," she admitted. "She's gone for the weekend."

Something flashed in his eyes. "Then you absolutely shouldn't be asking me up."

Her jaw jutted. He couldn't begin to understand that she was the adult of the family, not Lola. "Why not?"

One long finger rose, stroked only once down her cheek. "Because, pretty Cleo—" his voice turned husky "—you are just about more temptation than this man can resist."

She had an urge to close her eyes, soak in that touch. "Maybe—" Her voice cracked slightly. "Maybe you don't have to."

His smile spread slowly, heartbreakingly sexy. "Oh, yes. I surely do. You see, if I went up there, well, I'd have to tell my mama on myself. There'd be no choice."

Cleo burst out laughing, and the time-standing-still moment dissolved. "And how would she respond?"

"She'd be forced to take a new switch from the willow tree. It's a terrible sight, I promise you." Golden lights twinkled in the soft brown eyes.

Cleo couldn't quit grinning. "How big is your mother?"

"About two inches taller than you, but that's not the point. Going upstairs with you wouldn't be honorable."

Her smile vanished. "And you're an honorable man, aren't you, Malcolm?" she whispered.

She could drown in those brown velvet eyes.

Malcolm lowered his head, and Cleo sucked in a breath.

"I don't think my mama would mind if I kissed you good-night, though."

Cleo had no idea what to do. She'd never been kissed before.

His lips brushed across hers, and Cleo jumped.

"I have to keep my hands off you or I won't leave, so you just be still, all right?" he murmured.

Cleo nodded, her heart racing fast as a rabbit's.

He groaned faintly as, warm and surprisingly soft, his mouth pressed to hers. With exquisite gentleness, he sipped at her, nibbled at the corners. He slid his tongue against her lower lip, and Cleo moaned.

Malcolm jerked away. "You'd better go inside, sweetheart." His voice was raspy, his eyes hot.

"But—"

He shook his head. "Now, Cleo."

Reality landed between them with a thud. She didn't know him. He would be gone soon. She wasn't Lola, to flit from man to man.

Straightening her shoulders, she walked up the steps to her building. At the top, she turned back. "When you get home, tell your mama that you were a real gentleman."

Maybe he looked a little sad at that, but he didn't say anything, just nodded and waved.

Cleo reminded herself that falling for a tall, dark Texan wasn't in her game plan.

But when the tall, dark Texan showed up bright and early the next morning on her fire escape, waking her with taps on her window and flowers in his hand—

Cleo felt certain that her carefully laid plans would never be the same again.

CHAPTER FIVE

Present day

MALCOLM STARED out the smoked-glass windows of his office to the view of Town Lake. Nine stories below, runners and walkers filled the hike-and-bike path, while canoes dotted the still waters. A jogger with a racing stroller caught his eye and resurrected the thought that had danced at the edges of his mind all morning.

A baby. His baby. More than once, he'd been back in years long past, after he'd convinced Cleo to move to Austin and marry him. Remembering the day Cleo had called out his name, then picked her way, hugely pregnant, through the job site where Malcolm worked as a carpenter to support them while he finished school in the evening.

He could still recall the instant spurt of panic. "Now?"

Cleo nodded. "Now."

"Let's go. How often are they coming?" He was

pulling her along so fast she could barely keep up. Finally he swung her up into his arms.

"Put me down, Malcolm. We have time."

"I don't care. I want you safe." He slid her into the passenger seat, then rounded the hood.

"Malcolm, your toolbox." She pointed toward the job site. It had taken them months to buy all the tools he required, many of them at pawnshops. He couldn't afford to lose them. "You could probably finish out the day."

"We need the money, but—" He raked his fingers through his shoulder-length hair, then planted a kiss on her mouth. "We'll be fine. We haven't starved yet."

Her getting pregnant before they'd planned hadn't been easy, but Cleo's earlier life had prepared her well. She might look like the Snow White he affectionately called her, but she was no fairy-tale maiden. She could pinch a nickel until it screamed, knew all about making meals out of simple ingredients. In their little country rental house, they'd learned to garden and can the harvest. They belonged to a food co-op, which bought in bulk. She had worked as a waitress until she'd gotten too big to squeeze between the tables, and made them both clothes at night while Malcolm attended class or studied. She baked bread from flour she'd ground herself. Their baby's layette was a product of her own stitches, one much-loved garment at a time. Malcolm's family had wanted to help, but pride had only recently let them accept anything—his mother's old sewing machine when his mother had insisted she wanted a fancy new one.

"And we won't starve," Cleo responded, leaning against him. "Now, go pick up those tools and let's get on with bringing our baby into the world."

Almost twenty-four hours later, they were getting close. "Breathe, Snow, come on, keep the rhythm."

The pet name didn't buy him any goodwill just now. "This is your fault, you irresistible jerk."

Malcolm had been up for as many hours as she had, but from somewhere he found a chuckle. "We'll discuss that later, babe, but right now, you're going to pant."

She glared and gripped his hand so tightly he could have sworn his bones creaked. She panted, long past the relaxation they'd practiced in Lamaze class. When the agony slowed, she fell slack against the pillow, her head lolling. "I want drugs."

But nothing could budge Malcolm's good humor. "No, you don't. It was your idea—nothing unnatural in the baby's system." He kissed her temple and brushed back her sweat-soaked hair.

"Remember what they said about transition? That you'd begin yelling at me and that would mean we were close?"

For a second she seemed hopeful. Then her belly tightened into an angry mountain of pain, and she started to cry. "I can't do this, Malcolm."

He kept his tone calm despite the urge to panic. How much more of this could she take? "Yes, you can. You're the strongest person I've ever met. Now, just listen to me and breathe."

And damned if she didn't, summoning up the will to keep trying. At the end of the contraction, she fell limp against him.

He stroked her hair. "Think about our baby, Snow. You'll be holding her in your arms very soon."

"Him," she muttered.

The next one was already under way. He sought a distraction. "We can have boys later. I want a girl just like you."

"I have to push, Malcolm."

The doctor looked up from his examination. "Not quite yet, Mrs. Channing."

"Please," she whimpered.

"Come on, babe. Tiny pants, remember. Hold back through this one."

Cleo squeezed her eyes shut and clutched at Malcolm as though it meant life or death.

"The head is crowning!" the doctor exclaimed. "Okay—push!"

Everything melted together in a cacophony of voices and pain and Cleo's scream. Through it all, Malcolm somehow managed to keep talking to her.

"The baby's head is out. Now, once more to get the shoulders through," the doctor urged.

"Deep breath, okay, babe, one more time, you can do it."

With a groan torn from the depths of her, Cleo summoned the strength for one last push.

The room rang with shouts. "It's a girl!"

Malcolm sagged and pressed his lips against her hair. "You did it, Snow—" His voice broke. "You did it."

Then they waited to hear the one important sound. And it arrived, a shocked and angry wail.

"Let me see her," Cleo demanded.

"For just a minute—there are things we have to do."

Her arms trembled with exhaustion, so Malcolm slid his beneath them. The doctor laid the tiny creature, coated cheesy white and smeared pink with blood, into their waiting embrace.

Cleo curled protectively around their child. Tears plopped on the jet-black hair. "Oh, baby," she whispered. "Hello, sweetheart. I'm your mommy and this is your daddy and we're going to love you forever."

Malcolm lifted one hand, cupped it around their daughter's head and realized he was shaking. "Thank you, Cleo." He cleared his throat. "For this beautiful child. I'm going to protect both of you and never let anything hurt you, I swear it."

"What will you call her?" a nurse asked.

They'd thought long and hard. Cleo's most urgent requirement was simple—no frivolous, flamboyant names like Cleopatra. Going against the mood of the times where children were named Moonflower or Sunshine, she wanted something solid, a name to grow into, to wear with pride. If it had been a boy, he would have been David. But Malcolm had gotten his girl.

Just then, their daughter's eyes opened as though she was eager to hear, too. Cleo glanced at Malcolm, and he nodded back.

Her smile was tender and beautiful. "Hello, Victoria. Welcome to the world."

AFTER VICTORIA had been Betsey, small and dainty, always trying to be perfect. Cuddling against Malcolm's side as he read her a story, his own brown eyes watching him from a smaller face, her tiny hand patting his own as if to hold him there with her. So still, while her sister climbed up and down from the big chair a dozen times.

And the miracle of David, growing inside Cleo's belly. The girls were so much older then, Victoria ten and Betsey eight, that it was almost like having a first child, the experience fresh and new, yet familiar. He'd spent hours rubbing scented oils into Cleo's belly in the quiet time after the long, hectic days ended, the girls in bed asleep. Cleo had been feline in her sensuality then, luxuriating in his hands on her, in her hunger for him. The woman who was always alert, ever organized and poised on her toes, ready to race, had floated through those months, and Malcolm had floated with her.

And when he'd cradled his son in his arms for the first time, Malcolm had wept. They had shed tears together, and their love had seemed strong enough then to survive worlds colliding, hurricanes, floods…fire, wind and famine.

But guilt had undone them, in the end. Guilt, and its legacy of pain. And blame.

Malcolm shook his head and turned back to the contract he'd been evaluating. He had tried, through the day, to envision having that same idyll with Vanessa, that sense of completion.

He couldn't.

He attempted to imagine himself telling her,

Fine, it's up to you. Go on with the abortion. Treating the child as though it was merely a deal that fell through, a momentary idea quickly forgotten.

He couldn't do that, either.

A day ago, a week ago, he would have argued fiercely that a mother's needs had to carry more weight than a father's because hers was the body that would change forever, her life marked for all time by whatever path she chose.

It was common belief that a child wasn't real to a father until it was born, that bonding began only at that moment. But Malcolm knew better. He had felt his children tumble, listened for hours at Cleo's belly and talked to them, even sung to them, felt them kick him in the night.

Things weren't the same for men as women, he knew that. A father could walk through a day and not think about the unborn child for hours at a stretch; a mother could never forget for an instant. He wasn't the one to pee fifteen times a night or turn green at the smell of food cooking. He kept his familiar shape, did not become a stranger to his own feet.

But that didn't mean that a father wasn't fundamentally changed by his children. Some men walked away and left mothers and children hanging, but he could not believe they ever totally forgot, even then. And for a father like himself, the change was monumental, cellular. Life-transforming.

He might not have been the best; he was sure he had not been. Busy building a career and income with which to protect them, he had left much up to Cleo, had not tackled all that fathers did nowadays, when society understood better that two parents were needed. But he had not been an absentee dad. Every night, every weekend, he had been there. He had attended plays and dance recitals, had coached endless games of soccer and baseball.

But, paternal virtues aside, he *had* failed in the most fundamental way. He had not protected his family, had not managed everything right, so that in the end there was only one child left, and no family. David was lost forever. Victoria had vanished…been banished, perhaps, in the violent, angry clouds of blame and guilt that had suffocated them all. Only Betsey remained.

Until this child.

There had to be a way to make it fair to Vanessa and still give him the life of his baby. Malcolm leaned his head against the glass and begged for answers from a God he didn't trust.

His intercom buzzed. "Mr. Channing? Mrs. Channing on two."

Mrs. Channing? *Cleo?*

He snatched up the phone. "Cleo? What's wrong?" He hadn't heard from her in a very long time.

"Malcolm." The tone was amused, but he heard

something odd in her low voice. "Does something have to be wrong?"

"No, but you don't—" Maybe he'd imagined the strain. "It's been a long time." He sat down. "How are you?"

"I'm fine. How about you?" She was lying. He hadn't misheard. She was strung taut as piano wire.

He'd long ago lost the right to pry, but fresh on the heels of his memories, her voice sounded good to him, nerves or no. "Never better."

A ponderous silence fell.

Then they both spoke at once.

"Betsey's kids seem—"

"It's Victoria, she's—"

"What?" Malcolm wasn't sure he'd heard correctly. "Did you say Victoria?" His heart thumped once, hard. "Have you heard from her?"

"She showed up on my doorstep this morning."

"Why? Is she okay? Is she staying? What's—" He'd given up hope of seeing her again. Wasn't sure he'd ever be ready.

"I don't know why she's here, exactly." She sighed, and suddenly, they were parents again, united by a problem. "She hasn't changed, Malcolm. If anything, she's worse. She looks terrible, all starved and filthy." There was a pause. "She hates me, Malcolm. Still."

Cleo and Victoria. Oil and water. The too-sensitive child had grown into a teen bent on destruction. She stole. She drank. She lied. For every time Cleo had held out a hand to help, Victoria had slapped it away. He'd had only slightly better luck with the teenager who'd once been Daddy's girl.

"I could talk to her, see if she needs—" He raked fingers through his hair, gusting his breath out hard. "Hell, I don't know what to do with her, but I could try to get her settled somewhere. I might have an apartment empty in one of my projects. I, uh, don't have room at my place or I'd—"

"I understand. Betsey told me about—Vanessa, is it?"

Malcolm winced, viewing himself from the outside, through Cleo's eyes. She had a rapier wit and plied it with skill. It had been a game with them, people watching while Cleo made up stories to explain them.

Old guy needs young babe to make him feel he's still got it—that would be her take. The image turned his voice harsh and don't-go-there. "Vanessa Wainwright. She's a lobbyist. Bright woman." Who the hell was he defending, Vanessa or himself?

"I'm sure she's lovely. Blond, right?"

He'd always liked them blond and tall. Cleo had been the only brunette he'd ever dated, and she was tiny, to boot. He had no idea why he'd departed so far from the fantasy.

Except that he'd loved her, not them. She'd been like air and water and food. Necessary. Essential.

"Yeah." His jaw tightened. "Tall and beautiful."

"Young."

Now he remembered the worst of times, the ways they'd known just where to aim to hurt, to speed up the untangling of the bonds of love and time, strained past bearing by their guilt. By silence that built walls. By unforgiving memory.

"Yes." He sat up straighter, fingering the papers on his desk. "Listen, Cleo, I've got to get back to work. I'll see what I can do to take her off your hands." He focused on the contract, ready for goodbye.

Instead, he heard her exhale sharply. "Malcolm, wait." He could almost see her gnaw at that lower lip, her green eyes troubled, head ducked slightly in remorse. She'd always regretted it when her wit cut too close. "I'm sorry. It's none of my business. I'm sure she's lovely."

He could hear a *but* coming. "But?"

She chuckled softly. "I wish you'd forgotten more."

I haven't forgotten enough, Snow. His smile was wry. "Sorry." Then he pressed. "There's something else. What is it?"

"I honestly don't have any idea how to break this to you, so I'll just spit it out."

He frowned but said nothing.

"She has a child. A boy, about four. They've been living in her car, Malcolm. Our *grandson*. Benjy—Benjamin David."

The air in the room vanished. "My God." He fell back in his chair, trying to think past the flash fire in his brain. "Where is her—is she married?"

"I don't think so, but we didn't get that far." There was more; he could hear it in her pause. "Malcolm—" Her voice grew so faint he could barely hear her. "He looks just like David."

He couldn't speak. This day had delivered a broad range of emotion already. By the truckload. He'd awakened this morning with no sense that anything had changed. It was not yet noon, and his entire landscape had been altered.

He had a child who might die before he ever held it. His prodigal daughter had returned. He had a grandson, the image of the boy he still mourned. And Cleo, for good or for ill, would be back in his life.

"Malcolm? Are you there?"

He nodded, then realized she couldn't see him. "Yeah. Speechless, though."

And then he heard the low, husky laughter that

hadn't caressed his ears in aeons. "Tell me about it. I was barely awake and thought my worst problem was Lola doing Gypsy Rose Lee on the lawn."

Malcolm chuckled, his chest easing. "How is that wild woman?" Lola was an original. He'd always gotten a kick out of her, even though he often could not admit it. He was supposed to take Cleo's side. Now he didn't have to.

"More so than ever. Seventy-four is only a number to her. It has no bearing on who she believes she is."

"Gypsy today, huh?"

"Probably Ava tomorrow. God knows who by Friday."

And then they laughed together, and it was as sinful as sex. Forbidden and lovely.

"God. I can't believe it. May I drop by tonight to see him?"

"Be my guest. I'm not sure I'm going home."

"The house is filling up, isn't it? You always picked up strays. David learned it from you."

"That place was huge three months ago. Maybe you should save the apartment for me, not her. She and Lola will get along like gangbusters. They always did."

"Why now? What brought her back?" he mused.

"She won't say. I'm positive she would never darken my door unless it was her last hope. She's fierce about Benjy, but she won't be grateful. I know better than to expect that." Then he heard her voice falter. "He wanted to be certain I had enough milk before he took any, Malcolm."

He pinched the bridge of his nose. "Why didn't she tell us? Let us help?"

"Why should she think we would?"

And there it was, the pink elephant no one wants to admit is crowding the room.

"IT WASN'T my fault!" Victoria screamed at Cleo. "I didn't see the car." Chest heaving, eyes wild, she towered over Cleo, and Malcolm stepped closer, fearing she would harm her mother.

"You have never loved me. It was always the others. Perfect Betsey, then The Son, the boy I should have been."

"That's not true, Victoria." Cleo's face was paper-white. "We love you."

"Once, maybe. Not in a long time."

"Victoria, calm down. You have a problem. We can discuss it rationally."

"Rationally? When you hate the very sight of me? When all you can think is how much you wish it had been me instead of him?"

In that one instant before Cleo denied it, he knew his daughter had seen it, too. Knew it because he had asked God the same question—why?

Why David, the good child? Why was Victoria so out of control, so filled with hate and contempt, yet she was allowed to survive?

They didn't wish Victoria dead, either of them. But they were desperate for her to stop hurting them, quit tearing the family apart when they were already bleeding to death.

And they wanted David back. Unlike Abraham, they cried out to God to ask why He must take their son.

She asked for forgiveness they couldn't convey. Needed to be told it was not her fault.

But it was.

And she had seen all that in her mother's eyes. Confirmed it by looking at Malcolm.

As long as he lived, he would never forget the way her whole body had sagged into acceptance. Hunched over and refused comfort they didn't have to give anyway. They were making it through one day at a time, one minute, one second, by pretending it didn't hurt to breathe. That everything didn't seem pointless. That they weren't lying in bed each night, unable to touch or comfort or share anything but the bare-bones need to survive when they wished they had another choice.

And the next morning they had risen to find her gone.

"AH, CLEO, I wish—" He didn't have to finish. She understood the regrets as well as he.

"Me, too. Except I haven't a clue what to hope for now, not really." She was silent for a moment. "Come see him whenever you want to, Malcolm. I don't know how long she'll tolerate my rules, but I will not let her drink in that house."

"She'll just do it somewhere else."

"Then I'll take Benjy away from her." Her voice was low and fierce. "I won't let another child die."

For a moment of insanity, Malcolm longed to tell Cleo about the baby. She was the only person who would really understand how he felt.

And the person it would hurt the most to hear.

A dart of sympathy shot through him, and she would hate that the worst. He couldn't help feeling it, though; Cleo was a wonderful mother. That a man could still father a child long after his mate's fertile days were over was a cruel trick of nature.

But Cleo wasn't his mate anymore. They simply had a mutual problem. "I'll go over there in a while and talk to her, feel her out on her plans."

"I mean it, Malcolm. That child is too precious. He deserves better."

"She's his mother, Cleo. A mother's rights count for something." Malcolm shook his head at the irony of that statement, coming from him, today of all days.

"The child's needs have to count for more. I'll give it time, but if I see that she's harming him—"

"She could run again and take him with her."

Cleo's voice went ice-cold, and she bit out every word. "I am not going to let her hurt him."

"Easy, Cleo. We don't have enough information yet."

"I didn't call you for advice. I merely felt you should be notified. I've been handling things by myself for a long time now."

Malcolm forced himself to take it slow. "You have. But like it or not, I am Victoria's father and that boy's grandfather."

"Benjy." Her tone turned sharp. "And she wants to be called Ria."

David's pet name for her. For a minute, Malcolm couldn't breathe. "How could she?"

"Because she doesn't care how she hurts us."

"Don't—" Malcolm exhaled loudly, rubbing his temple. "I'm sorry. No more arguments. The cards have been dealt. The point is that we both have a place in their lives, and there's going to be enough tension without us being at odds. We've been civil up to now, and I'd like us to present a united front."

She seemed honestly curious, her tone almost

teasing. "And how do you suppose we might pull that off, Malcolm, since we disagreed about almost everything for twenty-eight years?"

He chuckled, and the tension vanished like morning fog at noon. "But we agreed on the important things, Snow." The ease with which the pet name escaped his lips was amazing.

He hoped she hadn't noticed. "Let's remember that Vic—Ria played us both in the past. I doubt that she's become less manipulative. But she's still our daughter and we've been given another chance. Let's see if we can pull it off this time." He didn't have to elaborate on the consequences of failure. They'd already paid the highest price a parent would ever be asked to bear.

"I'm not sure if I can survive failing again. He's adorable, Malcolm. And I don't want to fall short with her, either."

"Let's take it one step at a time. How much did you find out about her plans?"

Cleo sighed. "Almost nothing. Benjy was scared, being in a strange place, so I sidestepped the battle to keep from frightening him worse. It was time to open the shop, so I left. But Lola and Cammie were with her. Maybe they know what's going on."

"I'll drop by the shop after I visit them. Maybe we can grab dinner and talk?"

Her hesitation went on a moment too long.

"Never mind."

"It's not…it's just that—"

He didn't have to be there to see the way she licked her lower lip when she was nervous. He was shocked to his marrow when he felt himself stir at the image.

Whoa. Don't even go there. It's just all this talk of the past.

"Forget it. Bad idea. I can call you later." He glanced at his watch, ready to finish.

"Malcolm—" She seemed resigned. "You're right. We do have to figure out what to do. I can make you coffee."

"Whatever. I'll contact you later." He disconnected without waiting for her goodbye, wondering why he was so pissed.

All this thinking about mothers and babies, about a life he no longer led, was only an overload of memories. When he'd arisen this morning, he'd thought his world was set, that he and Vanessa would go on as normal. They'd attend the Longhorn game this weekend, hit a party after, make love and read papers on Sunday, then return to work and start another week.

He'd had so little family these last years, only Betsey and his two granddaughters. Now there was family out the wazoo, and most of it troubled.

Welcome to a new world, Malcolm.

But even as he shook his head, a kernel of excitement grew. A grandson needed a grandfather, especially if there was no man in his life. Malcolm still had a hard time thinking of himself as a grandfather—he felt too young. But all the same, he believed he was a good one.

A grandchild and a child, all in one day. And a daughter reappearing. Had to be some kind of record.

Malcolm hit the intercom. "Eleanor? I'm going out for a while. I'll check in for messages."

He strode out the door, hoping he'd find left inside his lost child, some remnant of the little girl who'd loved him.

CHAPTER SIX

DOWN THE ELEVATOR, past unacknowledged nods from security guards, Malcolm made his way to his car, his mind on the past. On a little girl they'd loved fiercely, though no amount had seemed enough. Betsey's arrival had occasioned the sibling jealousy in Vic that one would expect from a toddler, but David's birth several years later had been when the real problems had begun.

As he pulled out of the parking garage and threaded his way through heavy downtown traffic, he recalled the first time he'd realized how threatened Victoria felt about her place in their affections.

"Daddy, make her stop it!"

He'd glanced over his shoulder to where his elder daughter perched on one limb of the big old live oak in their backyard. "Vic, she's not hurting anything."

"But the tree house was my idea. We're building it, just you and me."

"Yes, it's our project, but Betsey can help. It's her tree house, too."

Victoria's lower lip trembled, her green eyes glistening. "Nothing is mine anymore."

Malcolm glanced from his string-bean ten-year-old to Betsey, two years younger. Tiny like Cleo, Betsey looked up at him with obvious trust that he would make things right. "Want to help me over here, Bets?"

The pink bow in her neat page boy shimmied as she nodded. "Okay, Daddy."

"But—" Victoria protested.

He stemmed a glare and forced himself to think. Vic had been so small when Betsey was born that she had no memory of how the demands of an infant upended an entire household. He placed one hand on Betsey's head. "Sweetheart, would you please get me a glass of ice water? I'm pretty thirsty."

Always eager to please, Betsey nodded. "Okay, Daddy." But where Vic would have run pell-mell toward the house, Betsey skipped daintily.

Malcolm laid down his tape measure and walked over to the branch where his eldest perched, looking thoroughly miserable. "Having a new baby has been hard on you, hasn't it?"

She glanced at him sideways, suspicious, then shrugged.

"We've expected a lot from you because you're the oldest. Your mom appreciates your help, and so do I."

She slid a little more toward him, her thin legs, with their perpetually scabbed knees, dangling from the branch.

"I know you get tired of sharing things with Betsey, and now there's David. I had three brothers and two sisters, and sometimes I got sick of never having anything to myself. I understand how you feel, but sweetie, that's what families do—they share. Good times and bad times, we go through it all together. We each have a part to play."

"David doesn't do anything. He just sleeps and cries and makes a mess. And we have to be quiet and Mommy spends all her time holding him." Her tone quivered with resentment. She was silent for a moment, then her voice dropped to a whisper. "If I was a boy, we wouldn't need him."

He should have realized she would think that. She was half-grown, so he'd assumed that she wouldn't fall prey to rivalry with an infant. But Victoria had always been edgy, had forever needed more. Malcolm lifted his arms and grasped her waist. "Come down here for a second."

Without hesitation she went into his embrace.

He put her on the ground, then settled on the grass, leaning back against the tree's thick trunk. Still holding her hand, he drew her onto his lap and wrapped her tightly in his arms. Stiff at first, she quickly relented, burrowing against his chest, her head tucked beneath his chin.

"Vic, I never wished you were a boy. You're my girl, remember? My special girl."

"Betsey's your girl, too."

Incisively smart, this one. He stifled a rueful grin. "She is, and I love her very much. But you're unique, Vic, because you were our first, something no one else can ever be. We three discovered lots of things together. Your mother cried when you were born because she wanted you so much. And you know what else?"

Tousled black locks shook beneath his chin.

"I cried, too."

Her head came up at that. "You? You never cry, Daddy."

He smiled. "Not very often. But that was a special time when you were born. You were so small and perfect and beautiful."

"Like Betsey is now."

He tapped her nose. "Like *you* are now."

"Mommy says I'm a mess. My clothes get dirty and I skin up my knees. Betsey's always clean and perfect."

Was there ever an answer that would satisfy them all? Kids scrutinized for the difference, sensitive in a manner that would do a safecracker proud as they felt for the most minute shift in parental balance. "Betsey and you aren't the same person."

Victoria snorted. "You can say that again."

"But one is not better. I love you both."

"Mommy loves her better. And now there's David...." Her eyes filled with tears again.

Malcolm turned her to face him squarely, holding her chin lightly between finger and thumb. "Vic, your mother loves you. Don't ever doubt that. She's just really busy and tired these days. Because she's nursing, she has to wake up every few hours to feed him. I can change his diapers and get up with him, but I can't nurse him for her. When he sleeps through the night, she'll get more rest. I promise this won't last long."

But he could tell that he still wasn't giving her what she craved, and it frustrated the hell out of him. Constantly in motion, half the time in a scrape of some sort, she had a restless spirit that drove her—and them—hard.

But she touched a tenderness in him that neither Betsey nor David, much as he loved them both, came near. Betsey was precious and—Vic was right-perfect. She would turn herself inside out to please Cleo and him, and Vic, too, for that matter. She was already eager to help with David and hovered over him like a mother hen.

And David. His son. He would be lying to say

that David's birth had not felt like a special blessing. Coming so long after the girls, when he and Cleo had almost accepted that they would have no more children, David seemed like a gift, a benediction upon their love. The doctors had told Cleo she could not attempt to bear a third child after eclampsia had endangered her life both times, and she had defied them and Malcolm, as well, to give him a son. There would be no other children for them, no matter Cleo's dreams of filling the house to the rafters.

But that was all right. They had three healthy, smart, beautiful kids. Figuring out how to handle all of them would be challenge enough.

And this one, green eyes ready to seek out his slightest hypocrisy, would always be the toughest hurdle of all. Malcolm acknowledged it, just as he recognized that he had more patience with her than Cleo did. It was easier for him—he wasn't here all day with three kids.

"Look, sport. Let's make a deal. You and I have designed this tree house, and we'll do most of the building because we planned it. We're going to find a special spot inside it, and we'll carve a note that Victoria Channing designed this structure. We'll put it somewhere that only you and I know. It will be our secret. Even though you'll share this house with Betsey and David, once he's old enough, there will be a part of it that will belong only to you. What do you think?"

Green eyes glowed, and he wished that she could see how much she looked like her mother then. "What would it say?"

"That's for you to decide. You design it the way you want it, all right?"

"Just you and me?"

"You're Daddy's special girl, aren't you?"

She ducked her chin and nodded shyly.

"Just you and me, sport." He hugged her, relishing the feel of her thin arms creeping around his neck to give him a squeeze.

"I love you, Daddy."

"I love you, too. I always will."

She leaned back. "I guess Betsey can help then."

He smiled. "That's my girl."

MALCOLM EMERGED from the car and paused, trying to remember how much time had elapsed since his last visit to this house that was once home. At least two years, he thought, for his elder granddaughter's birthday party. How could it be? When once this had been his refuge, his treasure, how had it all come apart?

Vic had vanished only three weeks after David's death, and since she hadn't been a minor, her case was low priority with the authorities. He'd hired a private detective, with no better luck.

Cleo had retreated into her own world and barely spoken. Only the need to keep a roof over the heads of his remaining child and the wife who didn't want him anymore sent him to the office every day, searching for something, anything, to distract from watching his family crumble.

Malcolm stared at the house he'd left five years ago, his chest tight again. So much love twisted into such pain. He'd always felt smug that what he and Cleo had together could endure any threat the world could present.

He'd never imagined the danger coming from within.

A lump rose in his throat at the thought of it. The one true love of his life, begging him to save her by leaving her.

So he had, and finally, he'd gotten over her. She'd gone on without him.

And now they must deal together again for the sake of the child who had destroyed their dream.

He straightened and moved up the sidewalk, his focus fixed on the front door, his stomach twisting into knots.

But when he knocked, there was no answer. Another try, but still no one arrived.

Malcolm gripped the doorknob and twisted.

This might not be his house now, but it was still his family inside. The unlocked door gave way, and he stepped in.

"Victoria? Vic?" he called out.

Above, he heard splashes from the bath. He hastened his steps toward the staircase to his right. "Victoria?" He glanced upward.

And saw her, huddled on the floor against one wall.

"Vic—I mean, Ria."

She turned slowly. Stared with her mother's green eyes, though hers seemed ancient. Defeated.

He didn't know what to say, so he simply opened his arms.

"Daddy." Her voice was older, too. Weighed down by hopelessness.

"Come here, sweetheart." He held his breath, waiting.

Her gaze wavered then. At last, with painful slowness, she rose. Halted.

Then ran down the stairs into his embrace.

Malcolm felt the sharp bones of her frame and hoped he wouldn't betray his shock at her appearance. The last time he'd seen Vic—Ria—she'd been a wreck, but a well-fed wreck, at least. They'd all been under unbearable strain and she'd aged overnight as had they all, but her body had held the rounded curves of a young adult woman.

This bag of bones in his arms felt as though she'd crumble into dust if he held her too tightly.

Yet the years before adolescent hell rushed back to him with the force of a freight train. The little girl who'd followed him everywhere, who'd tried so hard to be just like him, who'd learned to hammer nails with her tongue sticking out from one side of her mouth in fierce concentration...it was that little girl Malcolm hugged to him, not the stranger she had become.

A wave of protectiveness for this lost child of his swept over him. They would begin again.

Ria trembled, and a sob erupted from her throat.

Malcolm tightened his arms around her, one hand stroking her choppy black hair. "Hey, there, Vic." He called her the old name of her childhood. "It's all right now. You're home. Everything's gonna be fine." She burrowed closer, and he blinked to clear his eyes.

Then he looked up.

And felt his heart literally stop.

Oh, God. Cleo was right. The boy could be David, come to life.

He stood at the top of the stairs, frozen, his black hair wet and spiking, his T-shirt damp as though he hadn't quite dried off.

It was all Malcolm could do to remain still and not charge the stairs to sweep him up in his arms.

Vic must have sensed the change in him because she straightened and swiped at her eyes.

"Who is that man, Mom? Did he make you cry?"

Malcolm wanted to laugh at the boy's glare. Or weep. Shout. He squeezed Vic's shoulder, then took the stairs two at a time until he neared the top, putting his head at the boy's level. "I'm your grandfather, Benjy. And I'm very glad you're here."

The boy studied him out of eyes Malcolm saw in the mirror every morning. Something slow and sweet rolled over in his chest.

"Lola has a dog named Tyrone," the boy said.

Malcolm grinned. "That old guy is still around?"

Benjy nodded. "Aunt Cammie and Lola are taking me and Tyrone to the park. If you won't make my mom upset any more, you can go, too."

"I wouldn't like to make your mom sad. She's my little girl, and I love her." Malcolm wanted to believe that the Fates had given them a second chance.

The boy's dark head cocked slightly, and Malcolm's hands itched to touch him. But he'd have to earn that first embrace.

He'd do it, by God.

"My mom's not a little girl."

"No, but she used to be your size."

Benjy was clearly skeptical.

"No kidding. She helped me build a tree house when she wasn't much older than you."

The eyes widened. "Where is it?"

"It was in the backyard." He pressed his advantage. "Want to go see if it's still there?"

The boy nodded, peering past Malcolm for approval.

Malcolm turned. His daughter, eyes swollen and red, frame filled with exhaustion, nodded back.

He smiled his thanks to her and held out his hands. "Well, no time like the present."

"I don't got my shoes on."

An age-old habit became useful once more. "How about a ride on my shoulders? Your mom liked that."

Benjy seemed delighted but wary. "I don't know how."

Malcolm's throat clogged. What else had this child missed out on? "Piece of cake." He shrugged off his suit coat and climbed to the top step to be on stable ground, then squatted. This wasn't the hug he wanted to claim, but it was a start. "Turn around, cowboy." He lifted the child and blessed every workout he'd ever done. Lifting forty or so pounds over his head had been easier twenty years ago.

Benjy gripped Malcolm's hair as Malcolm stood up. Malcolm placed his hands on the child's legs to stabilize him. "Okay, sport, here we go. Watch the landing. We might have to duck."

"Okay." Benjy's voice was small at first, then increased with his delight. "Wow, Mom, see how tall I am!" He leaned over, and Malcolm had to grab the banister to keep them steady. "What do I call you?"

Malcolm couldn't help the smile growing broader by the second. "I never had a grandson before. What do you think?"

"I never had a grandpa. Nana Cleo said I could call her what her granddaughters do."

"The girls call me Gramps, but you don't have to. Pick your own. There's no hurry." Malcolm reached the bottom step and looked at his daughter, wanting reassurance that he was right, that she would stay. That they had time.

But she was in no shape to do that, huddled with her arms wrapped around her, a shadow of the girl he'd known.

He tucked her stiff body against him. "Your mom would remember where the tree house was. Let's get her to help us."

It was the right thing to do. She softened into his hug, and he pressed a kiss to her hair.

"Come on, Mom, show us where it was."

Malcolm led them both through a house so filled with memories that his heart was sore, pummeled by too-sharp heartache, too-sweet joy. When they neared the doorway, he tightened his grip on Benjy's leg and ducked without letting go of his daughter.

Benjy squealed and jerked at Malcolm's hair. Ria actually uttered a tiny, breathy laugh.

Malcolm entered the kitchen, smiling at Lola and Aunt Cammie standing by the sink, mouths open and eyes wide. "Hello, ladies."

And kept on walking, before this moment could vanish.

"Wow, Gramps, that's a big tree!" Benjy exclaimed, leaning forward.

"Whoa, there." Malcolm barely caught the boy before he tumbled. Unaccustomed laughter fizzed up from a place inside him he'd thought long dead. "See what you think when you're up there."

"Really, Gramps? I want up on that one." One small finger pointed a good ten feet from the ground.

"Benjy—" Ria stopped.

Malcolm noted her expression of concern and smiled at her, but she only had eyes for her son. *Slow down,* he cautioned himself. *He's not your child.*

But…dear God. Once again the resemblance to David rocked him.

"So can I, Gramps, huh?"

Malcolm slid Benjy down over one shoulder and into his arms, tempted to keep the child close and never let loose. *Easy, now.* "Let's start with this one, shall we?"

Benjy appeared ready to protest. Malcolm didn't give him time. "Up you go." He boosted the boy onto the lowest limb of the old tree.

Benjy wobbled to one side. Ria gasped.

But Malcolm steadied him instantly. "Grab on with both hands."

"Maybe he should wait," Ria said.

"Gramps won't let me fall, will you?" His sturdy little body slid precariously as he craned to view above him, then below, his eyes sparkling. "Look, Mom, I'm way taller. I bet nobody's as high as I am."

He shifted suddenly to peer behind him.

Once more, he slipped. Malcolm stopped his descent. "If you're going to play in this tree, you have to take responsibility for yourself. Some falls can hurt you badly. One time David—" He stopped.

"That's my name, David," Benjy said.

Cleo had warned him, but for a second, Malcolm couldn't seem to get a breath. He glanced at Ria; anguish was there, but immediately she dropped her head. "Can you spot the tree house, Benjy?"

"Yeah. Wow, this is cool, Gramps. Can I climb up to the part that's left?"

"No." Ria answered him first. "It's too far up there. You're not ready."

His lower lip stuck out. "I can do it. I *can,* Mom."

"You've never climbed a tree before. Take it one step at a time."

"I'm not a baby. I'm big now."

"Benjy, don't argue with me. I said no, and that's that."

Benjy glared at her, his eyes watery, his lip trembling. "I hate you. You don't want me to do anything fun."

Ria reeled from the impact of his words. Shame and anger warred on her face. "Don't talk to your mother that way," Malcolm said. "She's only trying to watch over you. If you're truly big, then act accordingly."

Benjy's widened with shock. For a moment, his chin jutted out. Then he ducked his head. "I'm sorry."

"Not me. Apologize to your mother."

Tears trembled on his lashes. "I'm sorry, Mom." Then he sought out Malcolm. "Don't be mad at me."

Malcolm laid one hand on Benjy's leg. "I'm not, I promise. But don't ever tell people you love that you hate them, no matter how angry they make you. You never know if you'll have a chance to make amends."

He glanced at Ria, wondering if she, too, heard

past echoes of that awful phrase being carelessly hurled from her own lips. "Daddy, I—"

"Vic, sweetheart—"

A new voice rang out. "What in the world is going on?"

Malcolm glanced toward the house. "Hello, Betsey."

Ria turned to stone where she was.

His younger daughter stopped and stared. "Vicky? What are you doing here?" As always, Betsey was perfectly groomed, her dark hair in a sleek chignon, tiny pearls in her ears, crisp white cuffs and collar framing a black sweater, the perfect West Austin young matron. "You look dreadful."

Ria's gaze descended to her faded jeans and threadbare blue flannel shirt, her scuffed boots. Malcolm observed her through her sister's eyes, unkempt and painfully thin. "Betsey—" he cautioned.

But Ria's chin rose. "Thanks. Nice to see you, too."

Betsey's high, perfect cheekbones colored. "I'm sorry. I didn't mean—" She glanced over at Malcolm, then past him, her face a mask of shock. "Who—"

At the same time, Benjy stage-whispered, "Who's that lady?"

"Benjamin, my man—" Malcolm scooped him

off the limb and swung him in his arms. "This is your aunt, Betsey."

"What's an aunt?" he asked, blissfully unaware of the currents swirling around them.

Malcolm tickled him on the belly, and Benjy giggled. "She's your mother's sister."

"Oh." Benjy threw his arms around Malcolm's neck. "I love you, Gramps."

Tears stung Malcolm's eyes. "I love you, too."

Betsey choked. "You have a son?"

The horror in her voice brought Benjy's head around.

Malcolm wished for better circumstances to break the news to his youngest. No matter. The boy's existence was fact, and they would begin as they meant to go on. He was family and should not be punished for his mother's past. "This fine young man is Ria's son, Benjy." He fought a wince as he continued, "Benjamin David."

Betsey sucked in a gasp.

Malcolm raced past it. "We're trying to see how much work it'll require to restore the tree house to its former glory."

But Betsey wouldn't be deterred. "*Ria? David?* How could you?" Her head shook violently. "I don't understand. You show up after six years without a word and—you're staying?" She glared at

Malcolm. "And you're *smiling?* After what she put us all through?"

Betsey's face was bone-white and pinched, her gaze a tangle of anger and pain and yearning.

Malcolm resisted the urge to go to her, torn between his two daughters. But Betsey had so much more than her sister. "Watch what you say, honey." He nodded toward Benjy.

Betsey was beyond reason. "Daddy, how can you just accept this? Especially when he—" She pointed at Benjy. "When he is the image of—"

"Not now, sweetheart." Malcolm ceased swinging Benjy and pulled him up to rest against his chest, one hand protectively splayed over Benjy's back.

He ached for the girl who had been so softhearted and eager to please, who had traversed the rocky path between a troubled sister and an adored brother, always the easy child, the one whose needs came last.

That girl was nowhere in evidence, Betsey's usual composure unraveling, the eyes that were his own brown burning with a feverish glint. "I don't know what's going on, but I won't have it, do you understand me? You can't just drop back into our lives, when we were all settled, and expect us to act as if nothing ever happened." She shot him a devastated glance. "You destroyed this family, Vicky, and I won't let you do it again. We were doing fine without you."

"Stop it, Bets. Don't say things you don't mean," he warned.

"Oh, I'm serious about every word." She faced down her sister. "David was your fault, and Mother and Daddy's divorce was your doing, and I was left with no family at all. You ran out, and I had no choice but to handle it." Her chin lifted. "Well, I did. We don't miss you."

Malcolm understood her agony, but he couldn't let her continue. Benjy was growing frightened, and Ria was too fragile. "Elizabeth Anne, do not talk to your sister like that. If you can't be civil, then leave this house now."

Ria moved, finally. "No, I will. Benjy, come on."

"No, Ria." He held on to the boy, who stared at them all with wide, worried eyes. "Shh, Benjy. It's going to be all right." He stroked the child's dark hair.

"How can it ever be all right with *her* around, Daddy? She's never been anything but trouble. She broke your heart a hundred times. She killed—"

"Not one more word." Malcolm's voice was steel. "I will discuss this with you later." He gentled his tone. "I think it's best that you leave now if the situation is so uncomfortable for you."

Betsey reacted as if he'd slapped her. "All I want is for you to be happy. I've tried to fix—" She shot Ria a look that was incredulous. "Everything *she* destroyed. How can you stand here and tell me that I should go and she can stay here?"

Ria blinked rapidly as she stared down at her feet.

"Families forgive, honey. We have to go on from here."

"Daddy?" Betsey sounded so young. So hurt.

"Give her a chance, won't you?"

Betsey covered her mouth with one hand, tears streaking her cheeks, head shaking violently. She opened her mouth, but only an inarticulate cry emerged. She backed away.

Malcolm started to hand the boy to his mother and charge after her, but Benjy whimpered and clung. "Betsey, please—"

"I—" Her voice quivered. "I have to go now." A sob escaped. She whirled and ran unsteadily toward the gate that would lead to the front of the house.

"Daddy, I'm—"

So sorry. He could almost hear the words. He tore his attention from one daughter to face the other. Loneliness and fear rode Ria hard.

He ached for both his girls. He would seek out Betsey later, but for now, he would focus on Ria and her child. Holding Benjy on one hip, Malcolm gathered Ria against his chest.

She burrowed closer, still trembling. "I can't stay, Daddy. But I don't know where—"

"Shh, sweetheart." Heart heavy, he led them toward the house. "You need rest and food and time to think. It will all work out, I promise."

Please, he begged the Fates.

But it hadn't before. Instead, they'd lost everything.

MALCOLM LOCATED a parking place a block from Cleo's shop. With one hand on the door latch, he found himself reluctant to get out of his car. He hadn't seen Cleo in such a long time; maybe a phone call would be better.

Distance might help. Keep their conversation objective.

With a rueful head shake, he reminded himself that today's phone call hadn't gone all that smoothly.

Then the reason for his reluctance struck him.

He was scared.

Of Cleo? Not physically, of course. He outweighed her by nearly a hundred pounds. The top of her head barely reached his collarbone. Suddenly he could feel Cleo's breath warming the skin over his heart, soaking deep as he held her in his arms.

Shaken, Malcolm released his grip on the door handle and blindly peered out the windshield.

Recalled that final day. The last serious conversation he'd had with the woman he'd loved for more than half his life.

Could feel again how his legs had seemed weighted, his heart dragged down by despair. The way he'd braced himself to try one more time to reach her, to seek the miracle that would bring her back.

He'd approached the door to their bedroom, seen Cleo staring out the window. "Snow."

Words had deserted him in the futile campaign to re-create the world in which they'd lived and loved.

Once she would have turned to him, smiled, run into his arms.

Now she stiffened. Repelled every advance, holding on to herself as if, without vigilance, she'd fly apart.

Slowly revolving to face him, no longer supple and giving, embracing life…she was the stranger with whom he lived. Brittle. Polite.

The green eyes that had for years been his lodestone were careful. Quiet, dangerously so. His Cleo had never been quiet. Passionate, tempestuous, yes. Loving. Warm. Determined. Driven.

This woman was…hollow. Going through the motions, except for the moments she'd cling to their last child as if Betsey were all that grounded her to earth.

He'd done everything he could think of for eight months now.

And failed every single day.

Suddenly he was furious. Whatever happened to *for better or worse?* Where in their vows had been permission to vanish while still walking around?

"Betsey deserves more than this, Cleo."

She recoiled as if he'd slapped her. "What?"

"One child is dead." Merely saying that word nearly doubled him over. How could the laughing, beautiful boy be gone?

He shook his head to banish the question. "Another is missing. Even if you don't care about Vic, why are you abandoning Betsey?"

Her mouth fell open. "I'm not—"

For a second, he thought her old spirit would stir to life.

Then she looked away, and he saw her doing it again, composing that mask.

"Goddamn it, Cleo, stop this."

"What?"

"Don't you dare go away again when we need you."

She almost seemed ready to fire back, and he welcomed the fight. Anything was better than the robot she had become.

Instead, her face went blank and still.

How could he risk hurting her more? But how much longer could this go on? "I don't know who you are now."

A devastated glance. "Me, either."

An instant of communion. A flash of a chance. *Come back to me, Snow,* he wanted to beg, but a hard kernel of resentment got in the way. Who was she to put her grief before theirs? Did she think her pain any greater than Betsey's? Than his? She'd been the hard-ass with Vic, the one who couldn't see past the rebellion to the agony inside. He and Betsey had never quit trying. "I want to find her," he said. "I'm going to start a new search."

That shattered the careful facade. "Why?" Her voice was pure agony. "She murdered her brother."

"That's not true. You know it isn't. She didn't mean—"

"You were always too easy on her." Her eyes were lasers of accusation.

"You never loved her enough," he shot back.

"Of course I did, but she hated me." Cleo's whisper was as raw as a shout. "Her own mother. Why, Malcolm? Why?"

He moved toward her, drawn by her suffering. But she recoiled.

Never in all their years together had Cleo shied from his touch.

He stopped. Bled. "She didn't hate you."

Her eyes went bitter and hard. "She did, and she killed my baby to take her revenge."

It was he who withdrew then. "It was an accident, Cleo. What kind of mother would believe she ever intended it?"

She turned away. "A mother who failed."

"Snow, that's not true. You were a good mother."

He heard the past tense. She did, too.

"You still have a child here who needs you." He approached once more.

Again, she sidestepped. "I want you to leave, Malcolm."

His mouth fell open. "Leave?" he echoed. "For how long?"

She wouldn't face him, her back rigid, arms wrapped around her middle in protection.

From…him.

"I don't know," she murmured. "I don't know."

"You can't mean it."

But she only shrank farther into herself. "I do. If you care about me at all, let me be."

He watched her in stunned silence, unable to absorb that for the first time since they'd met on a cold San Francisco sidewalk, they were no longer one. That the woman who was life itself to him—and he to her—was damaged by his very presence.

What had they come to? It was more than he could take in, ravaged and bleeding himself.

"What about Betsey?" he finally ventured.

She rubbed her temples. "You're right. I...I'll pull myself together for her."

"But—" *What about me?* "Snow, how can you expect—"

"Never mind. It's not fair to ask of you. I'll be the one to move out. You're a better parent, anyway. You always were." She looked out the window again, her face a study in despair.

He comprehended then just how desperate she was to be away from him. Cleo loved every nail and floorboard in this house. Her deepest desire in life was to make a nest, to gather in her dear ones and provide them with the love and attention and stability she'd been denied growing up.

He cherished it, too, this place. Or had, back when they'd been a family.

But he loved her more.

"No." As he contemplated the enormity of his next step, his voice broke. "I'll...go."

Cleo cast him a grateful glance, and his heart shattered.

He almost begged then, but somehow he managed to do as she'd asked. Turn around. Walk away.

Out into a world from which their love had granted shelter. Peace.

Hope.

He'd been hanging on to a tiny scrap of faith

that time would heal them, that after a while they'd be shaky but, in the end, fine.

Unable to imagine that, just like Adam, he'd been cast from paradise.

But unlike Adam, he would find a way to return. He'd believed that with every fiber.

Instead, three months later, divorce papers were delivered to his office.

Someone got into the car parked next to his, and the noise jerked Malcolm from his reverie. He leaned his head back against the car seat, reminding himself that five years had passed. He'd built a life. Become a bigger success than ever.

Cleo was fine. He was fine. They'd gone on without each other. The journey to healing had been agonizing, but he'd done it. She had no power over him now.

And if you believe that, Malcolm Channing, you really are one hell of a salesman.

CHAPTER SEVEN

CLEO CONCENTRATED on the shelf of Victorian paperweights, fairly certain she'd already dusted this case, but Betsey's near hysteria, after she'd encountered Ria at the house with no warning, had taken her far too long to shake. It was past closing time. Malcolm hadn't called or shown. She should be heading home.

Tonight's plans had been irrevocably altered. There would be no interlude with Colin, and Cleo's disappointment was far sharper than she would have liked.

She should be glad she'd been saved from a foolish mistake by her prodigal daughter's appearance. Only now, though, when the opportunity had vanished, did she understand just how much she'd longed to experience passion again. Once her days had been rich with it. Full to overflowing.

Just then, a knock sounded at the locked front door. She turned.

There stood Malcolm.

Cleo froze, caught between the past and the future that had been whisked from her grasp. She drew a deep breath, smiled at her ex-husband and hoped he'd lost the ability to read her mind.

"Hello," she said, relocking the door behind him.

"I'm late—sorry."

This close to him, Cleo had to swallow hard at his impact. Older, yes, but still lean and powerful, his broad shoulders encased in an expensive charcoal suit that had to be Italian in design.

His young paramour must agree with him.

"You look terrific, Cleo."

"Thank you. So do you." How stilted they were. Cleo stirred herself to ask, "Still want some coffee?"

A slight frown creased his forehead as he watched her.

"Malcolm?"

"What?" He shook his head. "Sorry. Just woolgathering. Can I change your mind about dinner?"

"I—" This day was already too full of memories. "Probably not a good idea. I'd better head home soon."

He pursed his lips to argue, then exhaled. "All right. Coffee would be good. Thanks." He followed her toward the back. "You don't have to worry about hurrying, though. Ria's asleep, and Benjy is having a ball with Lola and Aunt Cammie. When I left, they were making sandwiches shaped like animals."

Ria. The name still stuck in her throat.

Cleo busied herself grinding Kona beans, struggling to forget they were Malcolm's favorite, too, and that Colin had roasted these for her himself. "What did you think of Benjy?" She kept her voice neutral. When he didn't answer, she peered over her shoulder.

To see him struggling with emotion.

"I—" His voice thickened. "Dear God, Cleo, when I saw him, I felt as though somebody had planted a big fist in my chest. I'm trying very hard to remember he's not David."

Fighting tears, she flipped the switch on the coffeemaker, but couldn't face him just yet. Instead, she reached for two mugs.

"I miss him so much." Malcolm's voice dropped lower. "It never seems to go away. Just when I believe I'm past it—"

Cleo pressed one hand to her mouth and squeezed her eyes shut. Silence pulsated in the tiny room, the throbbing beat of hearts never healed.

She couldn't quite manage to stifle her sob.

Malcolm came up behind her. Hesitated, when once he would have touched her. "Hey—"

The past was a whirlpool ready to suck her under. For a crazed instant, she longed to burrow into his arms. Return to the charmed world where she'd been so safe and happy.

But that existence had skidded to a screaming halt one night six years ago, and climbing out of the seductive embrace of despair had required all she had.

She was terrified of the memories Malcolm stirred to life. She could not survive hurting like that again. "Don't." She backed as far away as the small room would allow. "I'm sorry, Malcolm. It's—" She glanced to the side, to the floor—anywhere but him, helpless to explain. "Today has been—" Finally, she lifted her eyes, to see his wild with grief. Instantly shuttered.

"Yeah." Malcolm withdrew then. Stared out toward the front. In a moment, he cleared his throat and spoke again.

"Benjy's wonderful, Cleo." He smiled. "He went crazy over the old tree house. We're going to rebuild it this weekend, so he'll have a place to play. I told him I'd take him to the Zilker Park train, and he wants to see the Children's Museum, and—"

"Wait—" Cleo held up a hand, already suffocating from too many plans she'd had no hand in making. Her life had spiraled completely out of control. "What if I don't want that tree house rebuilt?"

He goggled. "What?"

"It's not your house anymore. You moved out, remember? You have a place of your own."

"You begged me to leave. You're the one who

filed for divorce." With visible effort, he snapped his mouth shut. Exhaled. Began again. "This is for Benjy, Cleo. Our grandson. How can you deny it to him after he's suffered God knows what kind of life with Ria?"

"They could be gone tomorrow, for all we can tell."

"Not if they have a real home."

"Then you take them to yours." Why was she saying that? She didn't want Benjy anywhere else, but she kept mum, her ire rising by the minute. Who were all these people who thought she was Grand Central Station or the Ritz? She'd had a life that she'd fought very hard to build. Now everyone was crowding in, destroying her refuge.

Malcolm's frown deepened, but something else hovered in his eyes. "I—I can't do that." He glanced away. "Not right now."

Leaden silence ensued.

"I told you I'd find them a place, but Benjy—if you could have seen him, how happy he was in that tree. And I thought maybe Ria could help, like before. She needs something to hold on to. A sense that she belongs. Some purpose."

"She was a child then, Malcolm. Not the hateful creature she became. We can't be sure that she's changed."

"You sound just like Betsey."

"She has a right to be upset."

"She doesn't have to be vicious. She was out for blood. I don't know what she told you, but she wanted to tear Ria limb from limb."

"Can you blame her? After all Victoria has cost us?" And here she was again, ripping apart the balance so hard won.

"She's your child, too."

"She hates me, Malcolm. She was always more yours than mine. Daddy's girl."

"She didn't mean for it to happen."

And suddenly, that chasm they could not cross yawned between them once more.

If you hadn't been so easy on her...

If you had loved her more...

The old accusations they'd brandished like daggers as each of them sought to battle past the agony and loss. *If only* was their silent chorus to guilt's melody. To the unanswerable question: *what could we have done to prevent it?*

Her voice was a stranger's, tight and shrill. "She took him to a party on the sly. She drank—a lot—and then she got behind the wheel of a car with a fourteen-year-old boy who adored her." Her breathing was harsh in her own ears. "She killed our son and walked away without a scratch. How are we supposed to live with that, Malcolm? How do we bear it?"

Malcolm looked at her for a long, charged moment. Then he shook his head. "The same way we've been doing for six years—one day at a time. We have a daughter who is dying by inches. Do we let her go, too?"

His voice hardened. "Turn your back on her if you wish, Cleo, but I won't." He made to leave. "I'll move them out of your house as soon as possible. I'd put them up in a hotel tonight, but I think that Benjy could use every bit of love he can get right now. I'd appreciate it if you could try to hide your contempt for his mother."

"I don't feel contempt for her. I just—"

"What, then? Disgust? Anger? She understands all that, Cleo. She's aware that you don't want her." His voice softened only slightly. "But she returned to the only place she had left to go, hoping that home was still there. You and Betsey have made it amply evident how wrong she was."

"Benjy can stay."

"Would you have accepted that, in her position?" Malcolm's eyes filled with pity. "They're a package deal. She may not be the daughter you wanted, but she loves that boy with everything in her." Brown hardened to agate. "She would never have come near if she didn't love him more than she fears you." His jaw flexed. "I'll explain to Benjy about the tree house. Goodbye, Cleo."

She watched him go, a man who walked just like the one she'd once loved more than life itself. Then she collapsed onto the flowered chintz sofa, weeping for all that she and that man had lost.

And would never recover.

A KNOCK SOUNDED at her back door.

"Cleo?" Colin.

She shrank into the cushions.

She didn't know how much time had passed while she wept.

"I can tell you're in there. I heard you crying. Let me in. Please."

She rose. Balked.

He spotted her. "I'm not after anything from you. Just let me—tell me who hurt you. I'd like to help."

The long day's welter of emotions had her too heartsick and weary to battle. How could she explain what she didn't understand herself? "Oh, Colin, I can't talk about it now. I can't—my heart—" *Hurts,* she thought, rubbing the heel of her hand against her chest.

"At least let me drive you home. You're too upset."

"Why would you want to be nice to me? I told you we can't—"

He laughed, but the sound was anything but

joyous. "As hard as it may be to conceive, I care about you as much as I lust after you, Cleo. I'm not as shallow as you seem to believe."

"You're not—" She sighed. "Oh, all right." She unlocked the door. "Come on in."

She sat down and rubbed at her neck. "I don't want to talk. I mean it. Just give me a minute to—" What did she want?

"Here." He walked behind the sofa. "Let your head fall forward. I give a hell of a neck massage."

"Oh, Colin, I don't think—"

"Good. Thinking makes you tense."

At first she couldn't relax, but after a few minutes, under the influence of his fingers and his humor, her tension drained away, replaced by sheer animal pleasure.

His fingers slid up her neck and through her hair, soothing the headache she'd battled all day. Cleo sighed.

Then he leaned closer. His lips grazed her throat just at that tender juncture of neck and shoulder.

And more than mere pleasure flooded through her.

He curled his fingers around hers and lifted them to his mouth.

Cleo's breath caught. Here was refuge. Kindness. More.

His fingers trailed down her arms, then back up the sides of her breasts. Faint feathering… slow, liquid heat. With exquisite care, he built the fire. Tended her with a gentleness that soothed the pain.

Alone. So alone. So cold, and here was warmth. Strength. Hope in a world that made no sense.

Colin slid his mouth along her throat with lazy, wet kisses that were a match to jet fuel. "Sweet… so sweet…"

She arched her back in unspoken invitation, alive again from the hunger of five long and lonely years without a man's touch. "Oh, Colin…"

He settled beside her. A kiss on her brow. Her eyes. Her nose. Cool air washed her midriff, chased away by the brush of hair, the wet heat of a mouth on her breast.

Cleo's eyes flew open, to see Colin's smiling with mischief. Her blouse was partly unfastened, her skirt halfway up her thighs.

Oh, Lord. She wasn't ready for him to see her naked.

She was torn between longing and reality, and her voice was harsher than she intended. "Don't." She pushed at his shoulders, jerked her blouse back together.

He was too beautiful. She was too old.

"Look at yourself through my eyes, Cleo. Don't run from this."

But she rose. Escaped. In the mirror on the wall, she caught a glimpse of herself and was shocked to her marrow.

She was a creature she'd forgotten, an earthy gypsy whose black hair tumbled over her shoulders, her mouth red and soft.

He stood behind her, hands on her shoulders. "Do you see her, Cleo? The woman who lives in your soul?" His fingers parted her blouse again, drawing it wide-open, revealing taut dark nipples, pale breasts ripe and swollen.

Cleo lifted her hands to cover herself, but he stopped her. "No. Look at what's real."

Once she had been proud of her body, had preened and pranced before Malcolm naked without a thought but to incite him.

Malcolm. Oh, God.

She yanked her blouse closed. Tucked it inside her skirt, focused on the floor. Sorting through violently seesawing emotions, she glanced to the side wall and saw the clock. "Oh, dear. I have to call Aunt Cammie."

She heard his quiet oath as she picked up the phone and dialed. Her aunt answered on the first ring.

"Aunt Cammie?"

"Cleo, are you all right?"

"Y-yes," she stammered. "I—I had paperwork to do. I'll be home soon."

"Did Betsey find you?"

The day crowded back in, suffocating the last traces of ecstasy. In its place burned shame. A trace of anger that the ecstasy had been so brief. "Yes, Betsey called me. And Malcolm came by."

Too many people stood in this room, in her head—Malcolm, Ria, Betsey, Benjy…

Colin and she were no longer alone.

"What?" She'd missed the question and Aunt Cammie repeated it. "Oh—no, I haven't eaten yet. But I'm not very hungry."

Except for what she couldn't have.

Then she frowned because she couldn't feel him in the room anymore. Cleo turned.

Colin was gone. Those moments might never have happened.

But they had. For a brief, bright flare, she had been someone she'd forgotten.

And she had felt beautiful, just as he'd said.

Her throat tightened and tears clouded her vision.

"I'll be there soon, I promise. Don't wait up for me. I know you've had a long day. Sleep well. I'll talk to you in the morning."

"You, too, dear."

She paused. Blinked rapidly, rubbing at her

chest. "Aunt Cammie?" Cleo wanted to reach out to someone who would care that her heart hurt.

But her aunt had already hung up. And Cleo was alone.

Again.

CHAPTER EIGHT

MALCOLM SAT in his darkened living room, staring out across the hills speckled with the twinkling lights of other homes…other lives….

Other families. Like he'd once had.

Like he'd given up when he walked away from the carnage of what had once been so full, so rich.

Cleo had gone on without him, had somehow surmounted the agony and built a new life. The woman who had once been the beat of his heart now marched only to the rhythm of her own. Betsey had grown up…David was no more…all of the bounty he had taken for granted had evaporated like mist.

Except Vic—Ria. Once again, he felt her tremble in his embrace, saw how shaky she was, how much her defiance covered fear.

Thought about her child. Remembered a tree house. Another dark-haired boy.

Malcolm smiled at a sudden memory. He'd been raking leaves in the backyard when he'd heard his son's voice.

"Daddy, Ria, watch this!"

"No, David, don't—" Victoria called out.

Malcolm looked up from raking just in time to see David leap from the tree branch into the pile of leaves below, easily six feet.

Fifteen-year-old Victoria got there before he could, tearing into the mound, her voice high and thin. "David, are you all right? Davey, talk to me!"

Malcolm skidded to a stop, his heart thudding. "Don't touch him—" he shouted.

She recoiled, but her feelings were the last thing on his mind just then. He brushed past her and fell to his knees, scanning the sturdy little body for injuries. "Can you talk to me, son?"

David's eyes fluttered, then opened in panic. He didn't speak, and it was a moment before Malcolm realized that he'd had the wind knocked out of him.

Cleo raced across the yard. "What happened? Is he all right?"

Just then, David sucked in a shuddery inhalation, followed by another, deeper one. He started to sit up, but Malcolm restrained him with one hand on his chest, then passed his hands over David's limbs. "Anything hurt?"

"I don't know." He took another unsteady breath. "Wow, Dad, did you see that?"

Cleo was beside them now, anxious eyes on David, hands touching his face. "What happened?"

"Your son decided to find out if he could fly."
The calm in his own voice surprised Malcolm.

"Oh, sweetie, tell me where you're hurt. No,
don't move."

Malcolm placed one hand on her arm. "Just let
him rest a minute. I think he's okay. Nothing seems
to be broken. Just got the breath knocked out of
him. Right, son?"

David grinned. Malcolm wondered if Cleo saw
the resemblance to the daredevil smile Vic had
once sported.

Vic. He didn't see her. "Where's Victoria?"

Cleo barely spared a glance, her focus on the boy
lying on a bed of leaves that had saved him from
serious injury. "She ran into the house, crying."

Malcolm sighed. A difficult childhood had become a worse adolescence. He reviewed his words
to her with chagrin. He'd only meant that she
shouldn't move David, but with that hair-trigger
sensitivity of hers, she'd been ready as always to
take offense.

David sat up, brushing leaves from his hair.
"Wow, that was kinda cool! I bet Ria never did that,
did she, Daddy?"

None of them understood David's hero wor-
ship of his oldest sister, but he'd been stuck to
her like a cocklebur since he could crawl. His
life was a quest to impress, to coax from her the

attention everyone else in the family lavished upon him.

Malcolm's temper frayed. "No, she was smarter than that. Do you understand that you could have broken your neck with that stunt?"

David was shocked, his eyes, so like Malcolm's own, grown huge and glistening with hurt. His mop of black hair stirred in the breeze.

"Your father's right. You scared us to death," Cleo said. "Don't ever do that again."

His lower lip trembled, all thrill of triumph gone from his face. "The pile was big, like my bed. I thought it would be like jumping on my mattress. But it wasn't. It didn't feel so good."

Cleo pulled him close, stroking his hair, her voice tangled between tears and laughter. "I guess not." She peered over his head at Malcolm, shrugging as if to ask what to do next.

Malcolm wanted to crush his son into his own arms, but better to make this a lesson the boy would remember. He had far too little sense of his own limits. "David, go to your room now. What you did was foolish and dangerous. I want you to stay there for an hour and think about what you did, the way you should have considered beforehand."

His son's expression was one of hurt. The boy was seldom punished for anything. His basic nature was easygoing, and there ran a bone-deep goodness within him. He was a child who loved to roughhouse with Malcolm, who played soccer with such abandon that he thrilled the coach and terrified his parents. But he also was forever bringing home strays: dogs, cats, birds, even humans. He had a heart as big as all outdoors, and he generally went out of his way to be thoughtful to everyone he met.

But the very similarity to Vic's recklessness worried Malcolm and, he was sure, Cleo, too. And the streak of rebellion he saw before him made him doubly intent on quashing those tendencies now. One Victoria in the family was quite enough.

"But, Daddy—"

It didn't help that Cleo also seemed torn, but she rallied to his cause. They'd always promised to back each other up and argue about it later if they disagreed. A solid front was essential with children.

"Your father's right, David. You're not to play with any toys. Lie down on your bed and reflect on this mistake."

David walked away with a heavy step.

"Look at him," Malcolm said.

Cleo turned into his side and slipped her arms around his waist. "Meanie," she teased.

Malcolm glanced down at her, his heart lifting at her tone. "He scared the hell out of me."

"Me, too." Then she giggled, covering her mouth. "What a dumb, dumb thing to do. What was he thinking?"

"That's the problem. He wasn't." Then he chuckled, sharing her relief from terror.

"I don't want him to hear me," Cleo laughed, pressing her face into Malcolm's chest.

He held her shaking shoulders, biting down on his own mirth as the small body dejectedly opened the back door. "Just a minute longer." He watched David's figure disappear into the house and the door close. "Okay, we're safe."

Cleo's beautiful green eyes glistened, her husky laughter going, as always, straight to his gut. As she caught his expression, her amusement faded. Her arms slid around his neck. "What's on your mind, Malcolm?"

As if she didn't know. "Just wondering exactly how soft those leaves are."

One delicate eyebrow arched. "Want to see?"

He played hard to get. "Probably scratchy." But he drew her behind the wide tree trunk.

Her tongue traced a glistening path around her lips. "Might get all dirty."

He lowered his mouth to hers. "Dirty is bad."

Slowly, she licked his lips now. "Tragic." Her hands slid beneath his sweatshirt, stroking his back, then around to his belly.

The fire that had never died shot through his veins. "Where's Betsey?"

"In her room, on the telephone as usual."

"Good." His hands slid beneath her sweatshirt, going suddenly still. "No bra?" he croaked.

Cleo's smile was wicked. "Makes it simple, doesn't it?"

Her breasts were plump, her nipples tight against his palms. Malcolm wanted to drop to his knees and taste them, but he wasn't sure he and Cleo were hidden quite enough. "How I want you. Why isn't it night? Why did we decide we needed kids? They're always awake."

Cleo arched her back and rubbed her breasts against his hands, her breath catching. "Don't know." Her eyelids fluttered downward.

Dropping the hem of her sweatshirt, he boosted her up to his shoulder. "You remember how to climb a tree, right?"

"Malcolm, what are you—?" Her green eyes danced. "In the tree house?"

"You got a better idea? Go on, climb."

She lost her hold once because she was giggling. "Aren't we too old for this?"

"God, I hope not."

"It would be easier if we used the ladder."

"You want to explain to the kids why we're playing in their tree house?"

She shinnied up another branch and into the window on the back side. "You'll never make it through here. You're too big."

"That stray dog was too large to make it through the gap in the fence when the neighbor's female was in heat, too." Malcolm scaled the limbs quickly, smiling at her through the window. With some wiggling, he fell inside, landing with a grunt. "Love can move mountains." He waggled his eyebrows.

"Lust, you mean." But she was already pulling off her sweatshirt.

"My dear Mrs. Channing, with you, the two are indistinguishable. I love you and I lust for you. So sue me."

Instead, she helped him undress.

BUT CLEO DESIRED him no more, loved him no longer. What kind of insanity had gripped him that he could have made sense of the steps that led him to this moment, to this sterile-cuckoo's-nest existence?

Ria needed him, though. Her child did, too. He had lost a family most would have called perfect—except for the daughter who wouldn't behave, wouldn't heal.

Now he had another chance.

The front door swung open, and Vanessa entered. In the moonlight slanting through the window, he caught her expression when she thought she was alone.

Pinched. Unhappy. Weary.

And, he reminded himself, pregnant with his child.

She was almost upon him before she realized she had company. "Oh—you frightened me." Her elegant forehead creased in a frown. "What are you doing, sitting in the dark?"

Malcolm reached for her hand and drew her closer, patting his lap. "Come here. Sit down and let me hold you."

He felt the moment of hesitation, as her native reserve warred with surprise.

"I don't—I'd like to change my clothes. It's been a long day."

With one quick tug, he could have her tumbling right into his lap. He'd like to hear about her day. Tell her about everything that rolled around inside him. Let her keen sense of detachment help him put it in perspective.

But the pinched expression had deepened, and she held herself very stiff, though she didn't retract her hand from his.

"Are you all right?"

She seemed startled. "What? Oh, yes. Fine."

"Vanessa, talk to me. I know you too well."

The gray eyes were cool now. "Do you, Malcolm?"

"What does that mean?"

"Do you really have any idea what I want from my life? How hard I've worked to get where I am?"

Malcolm let her fingers slip away and faced the windows, wondering what was the right thing to say.

"Malcolm? Are you listening?"

He turned back. "Yes."

"I can't take a sabbatical right now. There are two critical pieces of legislation that I must get through in the next session. I have a lot of work ahead of me, and I don't have time to be sick."

She had his full attention now. "What's wrong, babe? Have you been to the doctor?"

"No. And I'm not going. I cannot have this child, Malcolm. It's not—" She glanced away, her body tensed for attack.

"What are your symptoms? I'll call Dan Shapiro. He and I have played golf for years."

"Damn you, you're not listening to me. I cannot do this. I'm sick to my stomach all the time, I'm tired, I can't sleep."

He grasped her arms and pulled her into his chest. "Oh, babe, I understand that it's rough. Cleo didn't have many problems with the first, but with Betsey, she was—"

"Stop it!" She shoved at his chest. "I don't want

to hear about Earth Mother Cleo. I'm not her, Malcolm. I can do more than have babies. I hate this baby. I—"

She looked stricken, and he could see the toll her emotions were taking on her.

Then big, silent tears rolled down her cheeks, and she crumpled against him. The tall, cool, untouchable blonde collapsed into a doll with no stuffing. "I'm afraid, Malcolm," she whispered. "I have no idea how to do this. I feel so bad all the time, and I—" Her voice broke on a sob.

Malcolm did what he'd intended earlier; only, he didn't spill out his day. Instead, he sat in the big overstuffed chair with Vanessa on his lap, rubbing circles on her back while she cried.

And he thought about Ria, pregnant so far away from home, and hoped that someone, somewhere, had held her.

He murmured soothing words to Vanessa, unsure how many she heard. The same words he might have once murmured to Cleo.

For a moment, the elegant blonde transformed into a tiny brunette, and Malcolm was back in the house he missed so much, sitting on their sunporch and watching the trees. Telling the woman he loved that everything would be all right, thanking her for the beautiful baby he knew they would have.

He'd just gotten a child back, and a grandson to boot. Was he asking for too much to wish for this one, too? Especially since he would never love this child's mother as he should?

Malcolm tried to think of a way that he could give Vanessa his blessing to do what she wanted, to destroy the child they had made.

But he couldn't. Even if he were certain right now that it would lead to the worst pain a parent can experience, he could not spare himself. If he had to endure David's death a thousand times more, it would be worth it for the memories he had, for the feel of those small arms around him, for the pride as his son had shot upward to the promise of Malcolm's height.

For one Christmas-morning smile. One proud grin at an *A* on a report card. One night of making the monsters go away.

For all the love that had flooded him the first time he'd held each child in his arms.

She didn't have to want the baby. She could walk away without a backward glance, and he would never say a word. He would bear every cost, give whatever it took.

But he could not tell this woman it was okay to get rid of his baby.

I'm sorry, Vanessa, he thought. *If I could take your place, I would.*

Vanessa soughed one last, catchy breath and slipped into sleep in his arms.

And Malcolm prayed for the words to make things right.

CHAPTER NINE

THE LIGHT OVER the sink cast its warm glow on the deserted kitchen, once Cleo's favorite room in the house. It had become Aunt Cammie's domain and, little by little, pieces of her aunt's life had appeared. Delicate porcelain pitchers and African violets joined Cleo's bright Mexican pottery and gleaming copper pans.

Cleo surveyed the ivory walls, the Mexican tiles she'd laid herself, she and—

Malcolm.

She could still feel Colin's arms around her. For a few minutes, she'd experienced the forgotten luxury of someone to lean on. And a little of the magical tug of what might be.

But now, in her house under siege, Malcolm's handiwork everywhere around her, that tug felt like…betrayal. Cleo couldn't reconcile the woman Colin made her want to be with the woman who was supposed to be—what? Mother? Daughter? Wife?

No, not wife. And she shouldn't feel as if she'd

done anything wrong. Malcolm had probably never given her a second thought when he was inside Vanessa.

She pressed one finger to swollen lips, inhaled the scent of Colin on her skin. And mourned.

"Was he good?" Victoria's voice greeted her from the doorway, her spiky hair tousled from sleep, a crease on her face from the sheets.

"What?"

"No woman looks like that unless she's been with a man. Anyone I know?"

Cleo had put herself back together before leaving the shop, but guilt had her flaring back. "That's none of your business."

Her daughter laughed, sharp and grating. "It's true, isn't it? Who is he? My, my…maybe we have more in common than I thought. This is a whole new wrinkle, Mother." She strolled into the kitchen and leaned against the counter. "Want to tell me all about it?"

Cleo whirled on her, embarrassed and furious. "I don't have to explain anything about my life. You ran out six years ago and didn't have the courtesy to tell us you were alive."

"Am I supposed to believe you would have worried?"

"Of course we did," she cried, pointing in the direction of Benjy's bedroom. "That little—boy you kept him from us. Why? And what are you doing back now?"

"I thought—" Victoria shoved away from the counter. "It doesn't matter. I was wrong. You still don't give a damn about me. You're only upset that I didn't tell you about Benjy." She headed for the door. "Maybe he was better off unaware of you. I sure was."

"Victoria, I do—" *Care.*

But her daughter wasn't listening, gone from the room, leaving her disdain to ricochet around like a stray bullet, wreaking havoc.

What good had her caring ever done? Cleo could hardly remember the child for whom she'd had such dreams. So much heartrending love. Victoria was a living symbol of her failures as a mother. Cleo leaned against the opposite counter, rubbing her forehead, too weary to move. Somehow, she had to summon the strength to climb the stairs to her room. A shower, then fall into bed.

And hope that tomorrow would be better. Uneventful. The peace of this morning seemed light-years away.

Footsteps pounded down the stairs. Cleo moved to the doorway, to see Victoria pulling a sweater around her shoulders, fully dressed now.

"Where are you going?"

"Out."

"Where?"

Victoria's jaw was so tight the words barely slipped through. "I don't know, *Mother*. Do I have a curfew?"

"What about Benjy?"

Her daughter's laugh was bitter and sharp. "You'll take care of him, of course." She slipped halfway through the door. "And maybe, just maybe, you'll get real lucky and I won't come back. Then everything will be perfect in Cleo's little world."

"Victoria, I would never—" Cleo lunged for the door and jerked it open, but too late. Her daughter's long, runner's legs took her out of sight quickly.

I don't want you to go away, Cleo wanted to call out. *We can fix this.*

But there was no sense lying to either one of them.

SANDOR GOUGED a hole in the acacia he was carving and laid down his chisel in disgust.

He'd returned earlier, just in time to spot a thunderous Colin heading back to his place. He'd heard Cleo talking on the phone, then she'd slipped past his work area without her usual good-night. She was always thoughtful and respectful of his work, not presuming a right to enter without invitation, but never before had she failed to let him know she was leaving.

He wondered if he should intervene and warn Colin off. Cleo had had quite enough dumped on her lately, especially today. She was a remarkable human being whose beauty was more than her facade, and any man shallow enough not to see the whole of her did not deserve her.

How her ex-husband had let her go, Sandor could not imagine. He'd never met the man, but he scorned him. Betsey had told him of her father's much-younger companion, and Sandor considered it pathetic, if typical of men that age.

Sandor would not do that to his own woman. When he found her, the mate of his soul he refused to believe did not exist, he would guard her and cherish her and love her all his days.

Cleo deserved such care. Beyond her inner strength, there was a vulnerability that made him want to protect her. She was his friend, and she'd given him, new to this country, a chance to not only earn a wage but a place to practice his craft. There was nothing he wouldn't do for her.

He raked his fingers through already tousled hair and muttered a few choice words in Hungarian about the men in Cleo's life. Then he glanced over at the piece that held such promise and recognized that if he picked up his wood-carving tools again tonight, he would ruin the beauty locked inside it.

Perhaps a walk would clear out his head, so he could get back to work. Without pausing for a jacket, he strode outside.

Half an hour later, little more settled than when he'd begun, he noted that he'd reached Lamar and Twelfth, only a few short blocks from Cleo's house. He could hike up the hill and talk to her. See if she needed a friend.

But it was late, and he respected her privacy.

So he set out in the opposite direction. A short block down Twelfth, he crossed in front of a dingy bar that had withstood the gentrification taking place around it. For a moment, he contemplated entering to seek out a beer.

A scream cut through the darkness, emanating from the parking lot in back, he thought.

Sandor charged around the side of the building. Heard furious words he couldn't make out.

Then the sound of a slap, flesh upon flesh.

"Be still, damn you," a man's voice growled. "You asked for this."

"Let me go," a woman cried.

Sandor spotted them then, in front of a pickup, the woman half-naked and fighting. "Stop!" he called out.

They didn't seem to hear him. She clawed at the man's eyes.

He dropped her, and she slid to the ground with

a yelp, then scrambled to gather her things and retreated from him. "Get away from me!"

"Goddamn you, leadin' a man on like that. Come here."

"Let her be," Sandor ordered.

The man turned in fury. "Get the hell out of here."

"Not until I speak with the lady." Sandor cast a quick glimpse toward her.

The woman rapidly straightened her clothes, sobbing with each breath.

"Are you hurt?"

She glanced up then, eyes wild, hair choppy and short and black, face shadowed with fear and pain.

"This ain't your business," the other man growled. "Get back over here, Ria, and finish what you promised."

Ria? The man charged, and Sandor couldn't stop to ponder. He blocked the man's path, casting his eyes over his shoulder. "Go. Wait for me in front."

"You goddamn drunken whore, come back here!"

Sandor didn't pause to see where she went. "You deal with me now, unless you are too frightened of someone your size."

Mean eyes narrowed. "I'm not afraid of anyone." He took a swing.

Sandor had no trouble dodging that blow or the next. Each maneuver only increased the man's rage.

"Bring it on. You too chicken to stand and fight?"

Sandor ignored the taunt, watching for the opportunity.

Then it arose. He moved in under the man's guard, hooked a foot around his ankle and dropped him on his back on the pavement.

His opponent didn't stir, mouth gaping like a fish's as he sought the breath that had been knocked out of him.

Sandor chose mercy. "No man is worthy to call himself such if he mistreats women." He cast a disparaging glare, then turned to go.

He made it only a few feet before a bellow of rage preceded heavy footsteps. He whirled and met the charge.

Fists flew, and the skin on them broke. It was not his choice to continue the battle, but Sandor never backed down when trouble was brought to his door. He didn't choose physical violence as a means of resolution, but that didn't mean he couldn't.

"Break it up, you two," a voice shouted. "I've called the cops."

Sandor's opponent lifted his head, registered the situation and bellowed a violent curse. "This ain't over," he warned Sandor. "But you're not worth going to jail for, and she's sure as hell not."

With that, he took off running for his pickup. Tires squealed as he drove out the back way.

Sandor swiped at a cut on his mouth and glanced at the owner of the voice. "Is there a woman waiting in front?"

"The one who was all over that guy?" The older man shook his head. "Of course not. She's long gone. Best you make yourself scarce, too."

Sandor shook his head and wondered if he'd just encountered Cleo's bad-seed daughter.

CLEO AWOKE to the sound of a broken laugh.

Then a thud against her wall, followed by urgent whispers.

"Sorry, sorry." Giggles sliding up to hysterical pitch, quickly muffled.

She rose from the bed, heart sinking. This was too reminiscent of scenes she'd rather forget. With a sigh, she donned her robe and reached for the door.

"I—I'll take care of myself, Aunt Cammie." Despair threaded through her daughter's tone.

"You certainly will not." Aunt Cammie might be quiet, but she could hold her ground. "You think you're the only one who ever met hopeless, child? I'm going to put you to bed, and you don't be fretting any more tonight. Tomorrow is soon enough. Answers don't come that easy, not for most of us."

"They do for *her*."

Cleo clutched the door frame, knowing exactly who her daughter meant. If the idea weren't so absurd, it would be funny.

"No, they don't. Your mother just hides it better than most. Now, come on."

"I—I smell bad. This guy—"

"Shh, sweetheart. I'll draw you a nice bath downstairs where no one will hear you."

Ria's voice turned small. "I'm so tired, Aunt Cammie."

"Lean on me, child. There's love waiting for you to take it."

"Oh, Aunt Cammie…if only you were right." A world of sorrow and pain echoed in Ria's heartfelt sigh.

If only… How many times had they tried? How often had they failed to reach her, to love her right?

Cleo stayed where she was for a second too long, torn between hope and fear.

When she emerged, it was too late. They were almost out of sight, the tiny old woman shepherding a tall, broken child down the stairs.

While the tall child's mother watched. And wondered if she had the strength to risk having her heart broken one more time.

IN THE FAINT LIGHT of morning, Cleo thought she heard voices in the hallway outside her bedroom again. Rising from the bed, she pulled on her robe, then opened the door.

Benjy lay cuddled around Tyrone on the floor outside David's old bedroom. Solemn brown eyes gazed up at her.

Cleo smiled and crossed to him, then knelt beside the pair. "Are you all right, sweetie?" she whispered.

Benjy nodded, gaze worried. "My mom's asleep. I didn't mean to wake you up."

Cleo laid one hand on his head. "You didn't. I like to get up early."

The brown eyes lit. "Me, too." Then he petted the silvered black fur. "Tyrone visited me."

"Benjy," she said. He didn't know his way around yet, and he was so young. "If you wake up early, come to my room, all right? I really don't mind, even if I'm still asleep."

"Okay." A hand stroked the dog burrowed against him. "Tyrone likes me."

Cleo smiled. "Of course he does. We all do."

Long, dark eyelashes lifted. "You do?"

Her heart twisted. "Oh, yes, sweetie. We're your family, and we love you so much." A rush of tears pricked at her eyes. How alone had this child been? What had he seen?

She would make things different for him now. Better. "Are you hungry?"

Benjy shrugged. "A little."

"Let's put Tyrone out, and then I'll fix you something to eat, okay?"

Black hair bounced around his face as he nodded. "Okay." He lifted up his arms in a gesture so trusting that Cleo's heart ached.

She pulled him to his feet as she knelt before him. One hand pressed his head into her shoulder as she fell into an age-old rhythm, rocking him. Benjy's arms tightened around her neck, and Cleo inhaled the scent of little boy: salty, slightly acrid…infinitely precious.

Oh, God. So sweet. So painful. "I love you, Benjy," she choked out.

"I love you, Nana," his breathy voice answered.

Cleo squeezed her eyes shut to banish the tears that threatened anew. With effort, she rose, holding him to her side, and headed down the hallway, pausing before Ria's room to close the door.

Her daughter lay curled up on her side, clutching the bedspread in one hand, a faint frown on her too-thin face. She appeared so fragile and haunted…so in need of care.

A thousand times, Cleo had extended a hand to her firstborn.

A thousand times, it had been slapped away.

But what kind of mother stopped offering, regardless of the provocation, no matter how difficult the child? Where had the tiny girl gone, the one whose birth had seemed a miracle? The first step. The first word. Cleo had learned motherhood with the child inside this woman she barely knew.

No matter how far they'd drifted, couldn't she find a way to bridge the gap?

"You look sad, Nana."

Cleo tore her attention away from the woman in the bed. Placing one finger across her lips for quiet, she slowly closed the door and led Benjy down the stairs. Tyrone creaked along behind them.

When they reached the kitchen, Cleo opened the back door and let Tyrone outside. "Do you need to use the bathroom, Benjy?"

He shook his head. "I already did."

"You're a very big boy, aren't you?"

"Yeah. Gramps let me climb the tree yesterday and sit up there, all by myself. Did you know you have a house in the big tree?"

"Yes, sweetie. I do."

"And my mom helped build it? It's really cool. I was so tall up there."

Cleo remembered the excitement on Malcolm's face as he described their plans. "Gramps told me that you and he are going to rebuild it."

"Gramps is great. He knows all kinds of stuff. And he said my mom could help us."

She thought about the young Victoria, face

screwed up in concentration as she nailed the planks. Recalled her pride when it was finished. And Malcolm's.

"You want to work with us, Nana?"

"I'm not that good with a hammer."

He shrugged. "Gramps says he can teach me. I bet he can teach you, too."

She owed Malcolm an apology. Seeing Benjy's enthusiasm, she couldn't blame Malcolm for charging ahead with plans. She herself wanted to make up for every loss this child had suffered, wave a magic wand over his life.

So what if her orderly house was suddenly bursting with people? If her beloved tranquility was wrecked? Would she trade peace and quiet for this boy's eager smile, his glowing eyes?

In a heartbeat. "Gramps is good at lots of things. I guess I could try."

"Great!" Benjy squirmed on the counter where she'd set him. "Do you know how to make cinnamon toast, Nana?"

Cleo grinned and hugged him hard. How wonderful to have a child to care for again. "You better believe it. Want to help me?"

"Yeah!" Benjy threw his arms around her and squeezed. "I like it here." He pulled back, uncertain. "I wish we could stay," he whispered.

Cleo swallowed hard. "You can, Benjy." She

pressed him into her shoulder and stared sight-
lessly into the past, wishing for a different future.
"I really want you to."

Please, Victoria. Ria.
Help me find a way.

CHAPTER TEN

"MR. CHANNING?" His very proper receptionist, Eleanor, stood in the doorway to his office. "You have a visitor."

Malcolm glanced up from the stock profile on his computer screen. "Did I forget an appointment?"

"No. This one is…unexpected." An odd expression crossed her face. "Mrs. Channing."

"Cleo?" he echoed. "She's…here?" After the way they'd parted last night, *unexpected* didn't quite fill the bill. "I'll be right there."

"Certainly. I've offered her coffee, but she says it won't take long."

At last he pegged the expression. Protectiveness. Eleanor had begun working for him not long before the accident. Though he'd never shared his feelings with her, he was all too aware of how she'd shouldered extra burdens during those long months in the aftermath, when it was all he could do to put one foot in front of the other. She'd been the one to sign for the delivery of the divorce papers.

"No idea why she's here?"

Eleanor's mouth tightened. "I can tell her you're busy."

"No." He owed Cleo an apology. She must be completely overwhelmed by all that had happened. He'd stormed in with impulsive plans, as usual. Cleo was one for slow, careful moves. "I'm right behind you."

Eleanor's disapproval was evident to him, and when he entered the reception area, he could see that Cleo hadn't missed it, either.

She looked so small, standing there. So resolute.

He riffled through a handful of responses—*Why did you come? What do you want?*

Man, you're still beautiful.

He settled for "Good morning."

Nerves showed in her gaze, but she remained ramrod-straight. "Do you have a minute?"

His brave little soldier. "Sure. Eleanor said you didn't want coffee?"

"I have to get to the shop, but—" She held off until they were inside.

Malcolm shut the door and saw her shoulders relax slightly. "Are you all right?"

"Of course." She took in the room. Checked out his view. "This is nice. Very nice." Her fingers trailed idly over the mahogany desk. She'd always been so…tactile.

A vivid memory of those slim fingers stroking his flesh rocked him to the core.

"Cleo, why are you here?" His tone was too harsh, but no way was he explaining it to her.

She bit her plump lower lip in that way he'd seen her do a thousand times. He had to look away.

"It's all different, isn't it?" She glanced over her shoulder. "New address, high-rise building. Not one stick of the old furniture." Her smile was soft and sad. "Remember how you used to say you'd hit it big one day? You have, haven't you?"

"I guess so." He'd done well long before the accident, but it was true that he'd thrown himself totally into making money after they'd split up. Displaced all his pain and rage and longing into climbing the mountain of ambition.

Leaving behind him the gentle valley of peace and home and love. A poor trade, but all he'd been able to manage.

"I'm happy for you. You've always worked so hard."

She appeared to mean it, so why did he have a sour taste on his tongue?

He struggled to return the favor. "Your shop appears to be thriving. You've become a first-choice destination for the privileged set. Everywhere I go, women rave about The Jewel Box."

She shrugged. "Betsey's a big help." Her face

shuttered then, her mind likely traveling, as his was, to yesterday's confrontation between their two daughters.

"She'll get past it, Snow. She's got a good heart."

"Victoria got drunk last night." No prelude, no easing into it.

He closed his eyes. "Damn." He opened them again and rounded his desk. "I'll talk to her. And I'll get her out of there this week."

"No."

"What?"

"I don't want her to leave. Benjy told me this morning that he wished they could stay. He's such a love, Malcolm. I—" She averted her eyes. "It was my fault she stormed out last night. I have to do better." Green eyes locked on his. "And I will." A faint, rueful smile. "Somehow."

"Snow, she wants to love you."

She held up a hand. "Let's don't assume our usual positions on opposite sides of that issue." She paused. "I didn't drop by to tell you about her or to ask for help."

He waited, but she said nothing more. "Then why are you here?"

She compressed her lips, then exhaled. "To apologize. You were only seeking to do something good for both her and Benjy, and he's so excited about your plans. I have no right to sabotage them."

His heart warmed. "Don't sweat it. You had a lot thrown at you in one day's time."

"So did you."

She didn't know the half of it. "We're in this together, Snow."

She swallowed hard and glanced around the room, but not before he registered the glistening in her eyes. He was seized by an age-old urge to gather her near. Protect her.

But before he could act on it, she uttered a cry and crossed to his bookshelves.

He realized instantly what she'd seen.

Slowly, she extended her hand and wrapped slender fingers around the old wooden frame she'd rescued from a garage sale and refurbished. Inside was her first anniversary gift to him, a sketch of her deepest dream. The artwork wasn't highest caliber, but it came straight from her heart.

He'd bartered home repairs with an old wood carver, and for their second anniversary, he'd given her heart's wish back to her, carved into the headboard of the bed he'd made with his own hands.

Other women fantasized about fame or glory or wealth. Cleo's paradise was a house—only one, where she'd live forever—surrounded by trees. Small children, a dog, a cat. A woman. A man. One safe place, filled to the rafters with love.

They'd lived in that house; they'd had those

children—if not quite so many—and assorted dogs and cats, along with birds, snakes, mice and any other strays David could bring home.

They'd known that love.

And seen it lost.

Cleo drew the frame to her breast, head bowed and shoulders rounded as she clutched it against her. When finally she looked at him, her expression was stricken to the soul. "Oh, Malcolm."

He did go to her then, wrapping her in his arms and bending his head over hers, his own eyes stinging. Memory and love and pain raged through him, and he felt her tremble against him as they huddled together in a vain attempt to shield something unutterably precious.

He searched for words. "Snow…I—"

"No." She tore herself from his arms and backed to the door. "Please. I can't bear it." She whirled to go; then, as if only now remembering what she held in her hands, turned back. Thrust it at him.

He reached out but didn't grasp it yet. "Do—do you want it?" He wasn't sure what he wished for her to say.

She looked at it again, sorrow mingled with hunger. Her naked soul stared up at him through green eyes he'd loved for most of his life.

She tried to gather herself then; the effort was painful to watch.

"Snow, take it." *But you have the bed,* he nearly protested. *Leave me something.*

"No." With trembling hands, she returned it to the shelf. "It wouldn't be right," she whispered. "I made it for you."

His phone rang at that moment, startling them both. "Ignore it," he ordered.

But the spell of the moment was broken. Before his eyes, Cleo reassembled herself. "I should go." She composed herself in nearly military rigor. "But thank you."

"I'm sorry, Mr. Channing, but this is the call you've been waiting for from Ms. Wainwright," Eleanor said from the door. "I apologize, Mrs. Channing."

Vanessa. The timing stunk.

If he'd hoped Cleo wouldn't recognize the name, it was clear from her features that the hope was in vain. When she glanced back, her face was a polite stranger's. "No need for apology. I'd better get to work. Whenever you want to start on the tree house is fine with me, Malcolm. Make yourself at home."

He shouldn't have needed an invitation.

It is my home, Snow.

Or should be.

But no more.

Malcolm sighed. Watched her go.

Picked up the phone.

LATE THAT EVENING, Cleo drove into her increasingly crowded driveway. As soon as she stepped out of her car, she could hear the music. "Stop In The Name Of Love" played with loud, thumping fervor.

She nearly got back in and left. It had taken everything in her to survive the day.

But there was Benjy.

As she opened the side door to the kitchen, she made out Lola's unmistakable torch-singer voice, along with what was clearly a child's. The third singer's she didn't recognize.

Rounding the corner, she peered into the dining room and ground to a halt. In front of Cleo's long cherry-wood table, Lola belted out the tune, while Benjy stood in sock feet on the table behind her, brandishing a matching wooden spoon as a microphone. In the corner of the living room close by, Aunt Cammie pounded away at the piano.

The other voice was her daughter's, one Cleo had forgotten Victoria possessed, lost in years of rebellion and anger. Crystalline. Pure and lovely.

But that wasn't what held Cleo fast in surprise. It was the sparkle in her daughter's green eyes, the glow on her face.

Victoria was having fun. All of them were.

Wistfulness twined its way through Cleo's

heart, a moment's bittersweet longing to be playing with them. For an instant, she imagined joining the fun.

But just as she pictured herself taking her place
beside them, she knew better. She was no singer.
No dreamer. Lola and Victoria could ignore reality; she was the sensible one.

Her presence would spoil everything. So she
backed away.

The motion caught Victoria's eye, however, and
her daughter froze. Cleo tried to duck out of sight,
but Lola saw her next.

"Come on, hon." Lola waved her over with a
smile.

Benjy's face lit. "Nana, sing with us! We're the
Supremes."

Aunt Cammie kept playing, and Lola advanced
on Cleo, grasping her hand. "Here, take my mike.
I'm loud enough without one."

Cleo clasped the spoon in her hand, torn between the rush of heat to her face and a split-sec-
ond picture of herself in the middle of the group.

Belonging there.

She darted a glance at her daughter, afraid of the
derision she knew was waiting, remembering last
night's bitter exchange.

Victoria's body broadcast a mixed message.
The loose delight had vanished into tension, but

some of the sparkle lingered, and on her lips, the trace of a smile played.

Cleo was paralyzed by indecision.

Then Lola started singing again, and Benjy chimed in with his "woo woos," interrupting only to say, "Please, Nana."

Cleo stared at her daughter, waiting.

The moment spun out as if endless.

Then Victoria scooted over slightly to make room.

Cleo took her first deep breath, while a prayer of thanksgiving rushed to her lips. Gripping the wooden spoon as though her life hung in the balance, Cleo slipped into the magic, searching for a voice that was almost as unsteady as her knees.

DINNER THAT NIGHT was an island found after a shipwreck. The golden glow of shared joy bathed all of them in its light. Cleo tore lettuce for a salad while Aunt Cammie stirred the risotto and Lola sipped her wine and supervised. Victoria instructed Benjy on setting the silverware on the table.

Had someone been looking in the window at them, the scene would have seemed so…normal. Untroubled.

Cleo listened with one ear to Lola's tale of a former boyfriend in Florida, a lifeguard half her age, but her attention returned, again and again, to her daughter. Whatever the reason for the night's fragile peace, Cleo was too grateful to question it.

As she watched Victoria's patience with Benjy, Cleo saw a different daughter inside the skin of the rebel. For a moment, Cleo spun back into a rare memory of Victoria showing the same evenhandedness with David.

What had they been doing? She searched for the elusive wisp.

A present for Malcolm. A birdhouse David had wanted to build him. The project was almost finished the day Cleo found them in the tree house, intent upon their labors.

In the instant her presence had been felt, Victoria had metamorphosed before her eyes from tolerant guide to sullen teen.

Just now, Victoria stepped aside from the centerpiece she and Benjy were constructing, and Cleo gasped. The sound sent her daughter's head whipping around, and Cleo couldn't jerk her gaze away quickly enough.

"It's extraordinary, Vic—Ria," she stammered. "How lovely."

From mundane ingredients such as napkins and glasses and bread plates, her daughter had built a series of platforms in the center of the table. In each little niche, she and Benjy had placed a mélange of everyday fare—a handful of pecans in a small wooden bowl, an orphan glass filled with red and green nandina leaves, a rosy apple here, a golden pear there, fall leaves sprinkled like stardust in between. Assorted candles stood as sentinels.

All of it ordinary, yet the overall effect was stunning. Cleo wanted to elaborate but feared she might have already said too much.

Ria shrugged. "It's just…something I made up."

"It's beautiful. You have real style. None of those items is unusual by itself, but the composite is amazing."

Shy surprise was tainted by distrust. The shutters slammed down as before. Her daughter turned away. "Let's go wash our hands, Benjy. Dinner's nearly ready. Right, Aunt Cammie?"

"Yes, dear. Only a couple of minutes more."

The rejection sliced into Cleo's heart. For a moment there, she'd glimpsed a path to a new beginning, a way to behave as a real family, the dream she'd cherished during years spent following Lola wherever whim took them.

Almost her dream. Important pieces were missing. David and Betsey.

Malcolm.

Lola stopped beside her on the way to the table with drinks. "It's a start, doll." Then Lola, so free with physical gestures, set down one glass and hugged Cleo's shoulders. "Don't give up on her. She needs you more than any of us."

"I have no idea how to handle her. What to say."

"Yes, you do. You're a good mother, Cleo. You always were."

Cleo dropped her head and studied the tile countertop, while her eyes filled and her chest ached. "No. I'm not. I can't—"

"Nothing you really wanted has ever been out of your grasp, hon."

Fury sizzled up her spine. "I lost two children, Lola."

But Lola gave her no quarter. "You have one back now, and she brought you another. Are you going to run away when what you've longed for is here within reach?"

Exhaustion dragged at her. "Oh, Lola, it's not even close."

"I didn't raise a quitter."

Cleo's head jerked up. "You didn't raise anything, Lola. I raised myself."

But Lola only smiled, triumph in her eyes. "And you did a fine job of it, I must say."

Then Cleo saw her game. Anger had incinerated self-pity. She shook her head. "You are ruthless."

Lola picked up the glass and winked. "Why, thank you, doll."

Cleo returned to her salad, glancing at Aunt

Cammie, who was stirring madly, her face wreathed in joy.

During dinner, Cleo had cause to be thankful for a second time that Lola was present and a fount of stories. She kept the conversation going until dessert, though both Ria and Cleo said little.

But Cleo had been studying her daughter, and a kernel of an idea sprouted, maybe the next building block in a bridge to her child. "Ria, may I ask you a favor?"

Ria was startled. Wary. "What?"

All eyes but Benjy's were on them. He drove a little car around the edge of his plate.

Cleo swallowed hard. "I could use a new display at the shop. I'm curious if you would be interested in a job."

Ria seemed stunned. Cleo could already see the *no* forming.

She rushed ahead. "I'm shorthanded right now, and it's usually my responsibility, but if you could spare the time, it would free me to catch up on the paperwork that's been mounting because I've had to be out front more."

"Why?"

"One of my assistants quit, and Betsey only works two days a week."

"No, why me?"

Cleo gestured to the centerpiece. "I like your flair."

"Why would you trust me?"

Suspended halfway across a tightrope, Cleo felt her balance slipping. She cast a glance at Lola, intercepting her mother's chiding frown at Ria. Ria's expression was stormy.

Perhaps she should forget the whole idea, but even as she considered it, she saw the spark of interest in Ria's eyes. She had been about to say *because you're my daughter,* but perhaps they should stay a little more removed for now.

"We could make it a trial run. I'll pay you, of course, but if you enjoy the work and the display is effective, we could make it more permanent."

"Betsey will hate it."

"It's not Betsey's shop. And your sister will adjust."

"I may not be around long."

Cleo's heart thumped hard, but she forced herself to remain calm. "Even once would be a big help to me."

Silence spun out in an agony of waiting.

Finally, Ria spoke. "I don't have anywhere to leave Benjy."

"Cammie and I would love to baby-sit," Lola said, turning to Benjy. "Tyrone needs watching, and I think you're just the man for the job, Benjamin, don't you?"

Benjy smiled. "Sure, Grammy."

Cleo and Ria exchanged startled glances. *Grammy?* From the woman who refused to be called by anything but her stage name?

Lola sniffed regally, daring them to comment. "Then it's settled. Tomorrow your mother will go to the shop with Nana, and we'll have ourselves a gay old time."

Cleo looked at Ria. "I'd like to get started before the shop opens. Will eight or eight-thirty suit you?"

She couldn't read the expression on her daughter's face, but at last, Ria nodded. "I'll be ready." Then she rose from the table. "If you'll excuse us… Benjy, it's time for your bath."

When they had left the room, Cleo sank back in her chair, drained by the effort.

Aunt Cammie pressed a kiss to Cleo's hair.

And Lola winked broadly. "That's my girl."

THE NEXT DAY, Cleo locked the shop's front door and flipped the sign over to Closed, more tired than she could recall being in years. Ria had worked silently for hours, but the atmosphere had hummed with tension, and the effort to dispel it for the sake of her customers had been enormous. For a moment, the temptation to simply fall to the ground right then and there beckoned more strongly than she thought she could resist.

Cleo crossed the floor and came face-to-face

with Ria's display, a child's view of a Christmas tree from below. It pushed every button, tugged at the heart, sent the mind arrowing into a life no one actually led but everyone would want. She wondered how much of it came from Ria's deepest longings. This was the vision of a child wrapped in the arms of perfect love.

That life hadn't been Ria's, no matter how hard Cleo had tried. All Cleo had ever wanted was a normal, happy family life. The one she'd attempted to create had collapsed under the weight of her failure.

Right now it hurt more than Cleo could bear. She strode past the display and planted her mind firmly on her business. She would swing by the bank and deposit the day's receipts, then head to the market to pick up the items on Aunt Cammie's list.

One step at a time. One task at a time. It was the only way she knew.

She grabbed the bank bag and her purse, then made her way to the car. Once inside, she leaned her forehead against the window.

The tightrope was exhausting.

Briefly, she contemplated going over to Colin's for a coffee. Sandor wouldn't be back for a while and a sympathetic ear would be welcome.

But she and Colin had lost their footing. He didn't understand her about-face, and she couldn't explain what she didn't comprehend herself.

She should never have yielded, even that slight bit, to fancy. She might have lost not only a potential lover, but a cherished friend.

All of a sudden, Cleo craved the freedom to drive off and never return.

But that wasn't her way.

So she might as well go home.

An hour later, after the bank and grocery shopping, she rounded the corner to her house, and for an instant, she was thrown back into a treasured past.

On her front lawn, the man who had been her life played football with the boy who had been their precious, unexpected gift.

Her heart bloomed like roses after rain, the sweet redolence intoxicating, almost too rich to bear.

Then Malcolm turned, and she saw the silver in his hair, the lines on his face.

And with painful clarity, Cleo crashed back into the present.

He was not her love anymore. And that was not their love child.

But he'd kept her drawing.

Worn-out from the emotional tug-of-war, she stopped in the driveway and emerged from her car.

Benjy tore across the lawn, shouting, "Nana, look! Me and Gramps are playing football."

She knelt on the grass, and Benjy hurtled into her embrace. She inhaled the tangy smell of little boy and closed her eyes to savor the feel of his arms around her neck, his weight against her.

Then she opened her eyes, and there was Malcolm. His dark gaze was as haunted as the hollows of her heart.

Oh, Malcolm, where did we lose it? Why did we let it go? Why couldn't we comfort each other?

Her lips parted, the words thick and full and aching in her throat.

"Nana, I made a touchdown! Gramps couldn't catch me—could you, Gramps?"

Malcolm's gaze jerked away. "Too fast for me, sport." He grinned, eyebrows waggling. "But I'm feeling lucky now." He rubbed his hands together gleefully. "Let's see whatcha got, big guy. Bet you can't do it again."

Benjy tore off in a flash.

Malcolm helped her rise, his touch achingly familiar. Those moments in his office had paralyzed both of them.

"Snow," he began.

"Come on, Nana," Benjy called out. "Mom can be on my side and you can be with Gramps."

It was then that she noticed Ria standing on the porch. Ria stared at Malcolm's hand on her elbow. In her eyes was not the scorn Cleo expected. Instead, Ria seemed almost…wistful.

"Gramps, you ready? Nana?"

Cleo glanced away from her daughter. "Benjy, I'm sorry. I have groceries in the car, and Aunt Cammie's waiting for them."

"We'll help," Malcolm said. "We've got work to do, my man."

He reached inside the car and parceled out bags, saving the heaviest load for himself. Cleo held the front door, watching him turn and shove the car door closed with his foot, and once more, memory assaulted her.

Ria was bigger and Benjy smaller than the boy and girl who had once performed this chore. The man had silver in his hair and was no longer her husband.

But for a moment, it all felt so normal. So... right.

Malcolm stopped before her, nodding for her to precede him. "Beauty first, Snow."

Once she would have lifted to tiptoe and kissed that cheek with its five-o'clock shadow. That she could yearn to do it now rattled her as nothing had in a very long time.

So she shook her head. "No. Go ahead." She took a step backward and stared at the ground.

Malcolm started through, then paused, as if about to say something.

Cleo wanted him to speak almost as much as she wished he would go away.

"Daddy?"

They both jolted at Ria's voice. Malcolm was so close that Cleo could inhale the scent of him, once so beloved and reassuring.

"Would you stay and have supper with us? Aunt Cammie says there's plenty." Ria's voice sounded young. Uncertain. Pleading.

Malcolm cast Cleo a glance, granting her the final say.

"Mother? You don't mind, do you?" Her daughter's too-slight body tensed for disappointment.

Cleo didn't know what her answer would have been. Before she had a chance to respond, Malcolm did. "I'm sorry, Ria. I wish I could, but—"

He didn't have to speak the words. Suddenly, the young, beautiful woman Cleo had never met rose like a specter filling the room. Reminding her that all their memories were only that—old times ground into dust, ashes scattered on the wind.

Ria's shoulders drooped.

Cleo's back straightened as she wrangled her voice into brisk unconcern. "We'd better not monopolize any more of your time. Ria, why don't you take one of these bags and I'll carry the other, so Malcolm can go."

Malcolm's hand stopped hers as she reached for the sack nearest her. She was desperate to get out of the room that had abruptly turned airless.

"I'm sorry, Ria." His words were directed at their daughter, but his focus was squarely on Cleo, commanding her to look. "I really wish I could." He held her fast, dark eyes searching. And seemed truly remorseful.

Cleo dragged a breath into her starved lungs, fighting what he made her feel. Resenting that she, too, longed for him to stay. Despising the treacherous lure of their past.

Malcolm had his life, and she had hers. Ria's arrival had disturbed the order, and they would have to adjust, but they were both reasonable people, and they would.

Right now, though, she needed to be alone. Away from Malcolm's scent, from the pull of his dark eyes.

"Perhaps another time," she murmured.

With careful steps, Cleo headed for the kitchen.

CHAPTER ELEVEN

ON SUNDAY MORNING, Malcolm stood outside the red front door he'd installed for Cleo not long after they'd moved in. His hand was raised, but he wasn't sure he was ready. Knocking still seemed awkward and artificial when he had a personal relationship with almost every board and nail in this place.

But he didn't have a key anymore. Hadn't in years.

And he was crazy to be back here so soon. He could still see the chill in Vanessa's eyes when he'd told her he had made plans to work on the tree house with Benjy today.

She'd always been independent of him, that was what had attracted them to each other. She had her life; he had his.

But it wasn't peaceful or soothing, that distance. These days, they existed in a state of uneasy truce. She wouldn't let him hover or protect her. She refused to talk about the baby or to plan its future. Every night, she made it clear that she was his child's prisoner as she widened the canyon between them on the bed.

If he'd thought it would help, he'd have tried to figure out a way to postpone this project with Benjy, but Vanessa had told him that she would be going in to her office today to take advantage of the absence of ringing phones.

Damned if he did—damned if he didn't. Lazy weekend mornings in bed with coffee and the paper had never seemed farther away.

Cleo wouldn't welcome the intrusion, either, but it would be his most likely block of free time this week. Once, Sundays had been sacrosanct in this house. The Channings closed out the rest of the world and spent the day together, just the family. No phones answered; no outside obligations accepted.

Well, he wasn't part of Cleo's family now, but Ria and Benjy were his, too. If Cleo didn't like it, tough.

He rapped on the door, twice.

Cleo opened it herself, breathless, laughter sparking those emerald eyes. "Malcolm. Come on in. We're making animal pancakes. Want some?"

He followed her through the door stupidly, still trying to work past the slap to his senses. A fifty-one-year-old woman shouldn't be so damn beautiful, but Cleo would be stunning at eighty-five. His hand itched to grab her, to turn the wattage of that smile back his way. To bring her up against the body that had known hers for a lifetime. Had been her first.

But she was already headed back toward the kitchen, leaving him to trail in her wake as though he belonged here and wasn't a guest.

And for a vicious, unflattering moment, Malcolm wondered how many other men she'd welcomed here since the day he'd walked away. Cleo wouldn't be promiscuous, but she'd have plenty of offers.

He hated every blasted one of them. Cleo was his.

What on earth was he saying?

"Coffee's ready, if you'd like some. I ground Kona beans."

Now he noticed the nerves.

Malcolm had the urge to call her back, to ask for a time-out so they could talk.

Or to turn around and leave.

But he could already hear Benjy's voice and the sound of a chair scooting on the floor.

"Gramps!"

So Malcolm shoved away his wishes. They were too confusing, too much in conflict. Instead, he knelt and scooped the boy up for a quick hug. "Hey, sport, what's up?"

"Mom's in the shower, and me and Nana are making animal pancakes. Want some? I'm real good at Mickey Mouse. Wanna see?"

He lifted the boy to his shoulders and ducked as they passed through the door.

Memory assaulted him. Cleo at the big griddle that was part of the old Chambers stove she loved. A chair stood beside her just out of harm's way, a platform to hold a child not tall enough to see from the floor.

The smell of butter just this side of burning, of pancake batter turning golden. An apron he'd seen a thousand times wrapped around her trim waist, above the gentle swell of hips he'd loved holding in his hands.

Cleo smiled, and it was like hundreds of Sundays before in a life that had been everything he'd wanted. More than he'd dreamed. Until—

No. Not now. Today was for the living.

So Malcolm smiled back, and their gazes held. If they'd been alone…

But they weren't. Which should be a relief. He lifted Benjy from his shoulders and set him in the chair, then leaned over the boy's head to study the creations hissing on hot metal.

Letting his attention drift to her tender nape, left bare by the casual topknot Cleo wore. And smelling the faint tones of the scent that was ever and always Cleo, both sweet and sultry.

"Want that one, Gramps?"

Malcolm yanked at his thoughts and struggled

to concentrate. When Cleo swerved her head in his direction, he almost thought he saw faint color stain her cheeks.

"Gramps?"

"What?" He cleared his throat. "Isn't that your pancake? Have you already eaten?"

"Nope. We just got started."

"Then you go ahead, and I'll get a cup of coffee. The cook should get to sample first."

"Okay. But after that I'll fix you one, all right?"

Malcolm ruffled Benjy's hair and pressed a quick kiss to the top of his head. "I'm counting on it." He put distance between himself and Cleo, casting the question over his shoulder, "Want a cup, Snow?"

"Not—" She stopped.

"While you're cooking," he supplied.

Their eyes met. They shared another smile. And too many memories to count.

Cleo broke away first. She held a plate and let Benjy retrieve his pancake. Malcolm took a sip and burned his tongue, then cursed softly.

Cleo laughed, shaking her head. "Still so impatient." Her eyes met his, then skated away. She busied herself settling Benjy on a bar stool and getting him milk.

She filled the room. Every corner was painted with her essence. Here, second only to her beloved sunporch, was where Cleo lived and loved best.

Malcolm thought of moonlit nights, making love on the chaise and trying to keep quiet so the kids wouldn't hear. He could see Cleo's pale, smooth limbs. Feel her sweet softness beneath him, her hair gathered in his fists, her eyes alight with love.

Desire slapped him so hard he nearly dropped his cup.

He whirled to stare out the window over the sink, glad Cleo's back was to him.

"Gramps?"

What he felt was…impossible. Wrong, even.

No, not wrong. She was the mother of his children. His first love.

But now there was another child to consider. It didn't matter that he couldn't imagine having a baby with anyone but Cleo.

"Gramps?"

He realized that both Benjy and Cleo were staring at him. Shaking his head, Malcolm muttered something about checking the tree house and walked outside.

Fast.

"WHERE'S GRAMPS GOING?" Benjy asked. "Doesn't he want pancakes?"

Cleo watched Malcolm stride across the grass, her mind inexorably drawn to hundreds of memories of him moving over that same ground. Headed out to play with his children. Throwing a softball for the girls, shooting baskets with David.

Cutting the grass in shorts and bare, muscled chest.

Making love to her in the tree house.

"Nana?"

"What?" She blinked. Shook her head to clear it. "Oh, um, Gramps is probably just checking on the tree house to be sure he's ready to work with you today."

"Can I go out with him?"

The expression on Malcolm's face when he passed her—what did it mean? For a second, he'd almost looked as if—

No.

Could it be? Was it possible that he felt the pull, too?

He kept your drawing.

"Nana?"

Cleo jerked her gaze from the window. "Wha— oh, yes. I, uh, can't see why not. Go ask Gramps what he'd like for you to do." *He's here for Benjy, Cleo. Not you.*

Benjy raced outside, Tyrone waddling after.

"Gramps, is it okay if I come out, too?"

Malcolm turned at the sound, and broke into a huge grin, bending to swoop Benjy up and twirl him around and around. Benjy's giggles made Cleo laugh.

The expression on Malcolm's face stole her breath.

Happy. Young. The man she'd loved more than life.

Who'd said he'd love her forever.

For a quicksilver second, Cleo recalled the first time she and Malcolm had made love. How she'd had to convince him that it was all right not to wait, a complete role reversal for them.

Emotions had been so easy for the young man Malcolm had been. He'd thrown them around the way a profligate spends coins, never worrying about starving later. Never fearing what would come back. He'd always felt safe, always been secure. He didn't know the first thing about being all that stood guard against disaster. About the price of living by your whims.

That day, she'd realized that it didn't matter what was smart, what was scary. She loved him, needed who she was with him. No matter how she fought it, she was sure Malcolm was the one. It didn't make her the same as Lola if she gave herself to one man, did it? She wasn't trying to sleep her way into a career.

She steadied herself by looking at him, at those chocolate-brown eyes that she adored. This was

Malcolm. It would be fine. With trembling fingers, she brushed his shaggy mink hair back from his forehead. "Okay, I'm ready. I want to make love."

Malcolm blinked. Then he shook his head as though he was trying to wake up. "You…do?" His voice cracked.

A shaky laugh escaped her. "You don't?"

"No, I mean, hell, yes, I do, but—" He sat up straight, leaning away from her, his eyes narrowing. "Why?"

"What do you care? Besides, I'm behind the times—free love and all that. Maybe I don't want to be a dinosaur anymore. You should be happy."

"Cleo, look at me." His voice was so gentle, his eyes tender as he reached out and cupped her cheek. "But I do care. You're my dinosaur, and I love you, just as you are."

He loved her. Cleo closed her eyes to capture the moment. Malcolm might be easy with his affections, but he'd never said that word before. She hadn't realized how much she craved to hear it.

Cleo drew herself up on her knees and framed his face with her hands. "Then it's time."

But even then, his desire had battled with his integrity. "What about marriage, the house, the kids you want?"

"You don't have to marry me to make love with me, Malcolm. It's the sexual revolution, remember?"

"No." His voice was suddenly fierce. "Not for you, it isn't. Don't you dare sell yourself short. You're old-fashioned, but I love that about you. There won't be anyone else for me but you. I thought we should wait until you were older, until you'd seen more of life." He sighed. "It's selfish, but I can't seem to quit wanting you to discover those things with me." His dark eyes pinned her. "Marry me, Cleo."

And even when she'd agreed to his proposal, he'd tried to talk her into waiting to make love. Finally insisted that they take solemn vows first.

He'd swept her into his arms and carried her, his strides eating up the ground as he headed toward a grove of trees in the night-darkened park. She could still see the moonlight on the strong bones of his face, the beautiful mouth.

They'd pledged their lives to each other, secure in the unshakable nature of their love.

"Snow, I know you have doubts. You don't think I'm serious enough. But I never—" his voice grew fierce "—never let anyone down when I give my word. I don't promise what I don't mean." His eyes were as fierce as his voice. "Do you believe me? I won't be like your mother, Cleo. I'll take care of you. I swear you can trust me."

Cleo had barely been able to speak for the longing that clogged her throat. She'd yearned for this, more than for anything in her life. *Please,* she'd begged whatever fates might be listening, *let love be enough.*

Then, on a star-spattered night and a moon-woven blanket, Malcolm had laid her down and bared her body, covering her with his own heated skin. With joy and not a little fear, Cleo had relinquished both her virginity and the shell she'd built around her heart, daring to have faith that Malcolm would not be like all her mother's men, that he was The One Who Would Stay.

In the aftermath of loving, they'd both wept.

Cleo had believed she'd found the talisman to ward against loneliness. Love would be their charm against heartache, and together they would be strong enough to face anything.

Now she stared out her kitchen window and twisted a towel in her hands as she wondered if that girl could ever have believed the day would come when she would turn from that young man.

Much less beg him to go.

CHAPTER TWELVE

MONDAY EVENING, with everyone else in the kitchen when she arrived, Cleo had sneaked up to her room for a few moments of peace. The shop had been unusually busy, and in her spare moments, her mind had drifted too often to Malcolm's visit yesterday.

Her eye caught on the new brass headboard she'd bought to replace the one Malcolm had built for her. She ran her fingers over the metal and felt a subtle sense of shame.

Malcolm had saved her drawing, still displayed proudly. When she'd begun to toy with the idea of taking a lover, her first step had been to change her bed. Free herself from memories of the past.

This bed was pretty and feminine, linens and all, but seeing that drawing, she felt a renewed sense of loss.

The bed frame he'd made for her was safely stored in the cedar closet. Maybe she should see if Malcolm wanted it.

No. Malcolm's little honey would not sleep in Cleo's beautiful bed.

Restless, Cleo walked out on her sunporch and stared at the yard. The tree house. Benjy had been in heaven being with his grandfather, and Ria had spent hours helping them rebuild the sanctuary that she and her father had constructed so many years ago. Listening to the three of them talk and laugh had been a special kind of torture for her, the outsider.

Not that she hadn't been invited. Benjy had repeated his pleas for her to pitch in, and she still felt a spoilsport for refraining.

The problem was Malcolm. For five years, he'd been absent from her life, but for many more before that, he'd been everything. To her marrow, she'd wanted to join them, to be as near to him as the next breath.

But Malcolm wasn't hers anymore, and if occasionally he looked at her too long and stirred yearnings in her breast, well…

Cleo pinched the bridge of her nose and reminded herself forcibly that Malcolm lived with another woman. Made love to another—

Damn. She wanted to hate him for finding someone else when she hadn't. Couldn't.

"Nana?" Benjy called up the stairs, yanking her from memory lane. "Aunt Cammie says supper's ready."

A welcome interruption to thoughts racing in circles. "I'm on my way, sweetie."

Benjy waited for her at the bottom of the stairs. "You didn't say hi when you got home."

Those big brown eyes. His grandfather's eyes.

"I'm sorry, sweetheart. Nana just had to have a few minutes by herself." She leaned down to embrace him. "How was your day? I missed you."

"I missed you, too," he said shyly, and hugged her hard.

Oh, this precious child who asked for so little from anyone. Cleo shoved away all other concerns and focused on him. "Tell me everything you did."

Benjy obliged, full of the wonders of Grammy and Tyrone and Aunt Cammie. They joined the others, and he giggled while describing how Tyrone had sat at the base of the tree house and whimpered to come up.

"I bet I could teach him to climb if we had a dog ladder, Nana. Think Gramps would help me build one?"

Everyone at the table broke up at the image of Tyrone making his way up into the tree house. "I'm sure Gramps can figure out something." Cleo grinned at the idea.

Even Ria's eyes sparkled with answering mischief. "Daddy's going to love that challenge."

They shared the smiles of co-conspirators. It

was the closest Cleo and her daughter had come
to accord in many years.

In for a penny, in for a pound, she thought.
"We've sold a lot of merchandise off your display.
The way you evoked an old-fashioned Christmas
tree from a child's view looking up from beneath
elicits an emotional response. More than one person stayed there for a long time with a wistful expression on her face."

Ria ducked her head. After a pause, she spoke,
her voice quiet. "I had an idea for the corner window, but…the shop looks fine. You probably don't
need it."

"If you'd like to tackle the project, I'd be very
happy to have you do so. What did you have in
mind?"

Cautiously, Ria broached her concept, and Cleo
could readily visualize how stunning it would be,
a fantasy of snow and ice and winter magic, perfect for the window that faced the street.

"It sounds wonderful. Let's do it."

"Really?" Ria's usual guard dropped.

"Absolutely." For a few more golden minutes,
they spoke as allies instead of foes, and Cleo sa-
vored the rich pleasure of it. "Could you start tomorrow? We have most of what you need."

Ria hesitated. "Will—" She glanced down.
"Who's working tomorrow?"

Sympathy stirred. *Betsey.* "Perhaps that isn't the best day, but oh, how I'd love to have that up right away."

"I could—" Ria halted, then began again. "If you would be willing to let me, I could start it tonight, after Benjy's in bed." She toyed with her water glass.

"Oh, Ria, I don't think—" She'd stolen from Cleo's purse, all those years ago. To trust her with the shop…

Ria shoved back from the table, gripping her plate in white-knuckled hands. "I understand. Let's just forget it." She reached for Benjy's plate. "About ready for your bath, sweetie?"

"Ria." Cleo's voice was strained.

"Do I have to, Mom?" Benjy's face screwed up in a frown.

"Hurry up, Benjy," she snapped. With obvious effort, she composed herself and smiled at her son. "Let's fill it really high, so you can play whale, okay?"

Benjy's eyes widened. "Okay!"

"Get your pajamas, and I'll meet you in the bathroom in just a minute."

His chair slid backward in a rush. "I should show Gramps how long I can hold my breath. Can we call him, Mom?"

"Ria—"

Ria kept walking, still addressing Benjy. "I don't think Gramps can come tonight, but we'll talk to him about it the next time he's here. Deal?"

"Yeah!"

"All right, then head up those stairs."

He paused on the second step. "Wanna watch how long I can hold my breath, Nana?"

Cleo overlooked Ria's obvious reluctance. "I'd love to. Just let me visit with your mother for a minute, and I'll be there, too."

"Okay." He raced up the stairs.

"Ria." Cleo rose to follow her.

Her daughter stopped in the doorway to the kitchen but didn't turn. "What?"

Cleo pressed on, digging her nails into her palms. "If you really don't mind getting started tonight, I'll call to see if Sandor's still there working. If he is, he can let you in." She paused. Bit her lip. *Somehow, we have to break this cycle.* "Otherwise, I'll give you my key and the security code, and you can just leave the key on the kitchen counter if you return after I go to bed."

Ria crossed the few remaining steps and set the plates down. When she faced her mother, her expression was as strained and wary as Cleo felt.

"Thank you," Ria said softly, blinking hard. "I—I'll just get Benjy's bath started." She went upstairs.

"Brava, Cleopatra." In Lola's voice she heard honest admiration.

Aunt Cammie merely passed behind and kissed her hair.

Cleo stared after her daughter. *Please. Don't make me sorry.*

Then she went in search of her purse.

"I'LL GET IT! I bet it's Gramps," Benjy shouted the next afternoon.

Cleo finally had a full staff back and had taken time off to spend time with Benjy before Malcolm picked him up.

When Benjy pulled the door open, sure enough, there stood Malcolm.

But he wasn't alone. "Hi, Nana," Betsey's daughter Marguerite chortled, her perpetual mischievous grin shining. Her older sister, Elizabeth, was frozen in place, staring at Benjy, who had fallen silent himself.

"Hello, girls. What a lovely surprise! I haven't seen you in days." Cleo knelt beside Benjy, holding one arm around his waist as Marguerite left Malcolm's side to bestow a big hug.

Malcolm crouched and cast Cleo a nervous glance before addressing Benjy. "Hi, sport. I brought you a surprise. These are your cousins. Elizabeth is four, just like you."

He drew the girl closer, but Cleo could see that Betsey had had her influence.

"And this crazy cat is Marguerite. She's three."

Their younger granddaughter was already resisting Betsey's careful molding. She giggled and held up fingers curled like claws and said, "Meow." Then she extended one hand as if to scratch and hissed. Then giggled again.

Benjy responded in kind. "Woof, woof," he answered.

Marguerite's eyes lit. She charged through the living room. Benjy was quick to follow.

Malcolm grinned at Cleo.

The cacophony of cat-and-dog sounds, accompanied by pounding feet, approached the level of pain. Malcolm rose from his crouch. "I'll go play traffic cop. Elizabeth, why don't you talk Nana into accompanying us to the park?"

"Please, Nana?" Elizabeth squeezed Cleo's neck. "Gramps says we can go for ice cream after."

The offer was tempting. Just then, Malcolm reentered the room. Animal noises segued to unbridled laughter as Malcolm swung them in circles.

He'd been a magnificent father. As a grandfather, he was even better, and Cleo couldn't help chuckling at the mischief on his face. Marguerite came by hers honestly.

He set them both down. "Nana Cleo is really smart, don't you think?"

All three children nodded.

"So that must mean that she would never pass up a chance to go to the park and then for ice cream, right?" Malcolm's expression gleamed with a combination of dare and enticement, just as it had a thousand times before.

"You're going to ruin their supper."

"So we'll get ice cream first, then let them work it off. Anyway, what are grandfathers for?" He grinned. "Give in, Snow. Live a little. Help me spoil them rotten."

She threw up her hands, feeling about sixteen. Seventeen, actually—and invigorated by smiling dark eyes and a cold San Francisco breeze on the night that had changed her life forever. "All right, all right. Let me switch my shoes."

The chorus of cheers warmed her.

But it was Malcolm's smile that stayed with her all the way upstairs to her room.

AN HOUR LATER, they sat on a bench, watching the children at the monkey bars. Elizabeth remained on the ground, while Marguerite was already at the top level, with Benjy not far behind.

Suddenly Benjy looked back. He reversed his

progress until he'd gone halfway. "Elizabeth, we can't let a little kid beat us."

And just that quickly, they were a team.

Leaning forward, elbows on his knees, Malcolm swiveled his head toward Cleo. "That boy's going a long way in life."

"Reminds me of someone else who could talk the birds out of the trees."

Her face was alive with memory and a fondness he hadn't known how much he'd missed. Then she shivered, and he realized that the sun was nearing the horizon. "Cold?"

She shook her head, but then trembled again.

Before he could consider the wisdom of it, Malcolm slipped an arm around her shoulders.

And for a moment, he thought she might let him.

He saw awareness hit her. She retreated and wrapped her arms around herself, so he did the next best thing and unbuttoned his flannel shirt, then draped it over her shoulders.

"You only have a T-shirt, Malcolm." She started to give the shirt back. "You'll freeze."

"In Austin in November?" He snorted. "Who was it who insisted that my thermostat always ran hot?"

And there they were, tossed back in time to so many winter nights when they'd laughed over Cleo's cold feet and hands, over how she'd cuddle to share his warmth and he'd gasp with the first icy contact of her toes.

All he could do was stare at her, his breath stuck somewhere in his chest. Their careful distance had vaporized. He wanted to touch her, to wrap her up in his embrace.

She looked as shaken as he felt.

Malcolm rubbed his hands down his thighs and pushed up to his feet, stuffing his hands in his pockets while he stared at the playground…and saw nothing. "I, uh, maybe we'd better get going."

Cleo rose, too, but stepped a careful distance away. "Girls, Benjy, time to go."

She picked a path across the gravel, her hips swaying slightly with that same sensuous grace that had made his blood run hot for years.

And still did.

He wanted to laugh at himself, except it wasn't funny, not one bit. He lived with another woman and had a child on the way. It was a hell of a time for his heart to be stirring back to life. To be learning that his wife still held it in her slender hands.

His *ex-wife,* Malcolm reminded himself. But his damn foolish heart didn't seem to be listening. He pulled his car keys from his pocket. "Okay, girls. Your mother is probably already waiting at my house."

ONCE THEY'D DROPPED Cleo and Benjy off, Malcolm drove into his garage, only halfway listening to the girls giggle and chatter. Vanessa's car was parked in her space; she was home early for a change. Betsey's vehicle was out on the street.

"Gramps, can we get Benjy tomorrow and go to the park again?" Marguerite and he were fast friends now.

He smiled. "Not tomorrow, but perhaps this weekend we can cook something up. What would you think, Elizabeth?"

She nodded. "Nana said we might have a slumber party, if Mommy says okay. You could come, too, Gramps."

Ah, the innocence of children. He pushed open the door to the utility room and watched them race through, thinking about what Cleo would say if he showed up for a slumber party at her house.

He was still smiling as he entered the living room. The girls chattered on to their mother, but he could feel the tension.

It only took a glimpse of Vanessa's pale and set face, then at Betsey's stiffness, to guess what had happened.

He would have bet the farm that Vanessa would never tell anyone. But however it had evolved, Betsey knew about the baby now.

And she didn't like it one bit.

"Hi," he said. "Sorry we're late."

"Mommy, we met Benjy and he went with us to get ice cream and play in the park," Marguerite enthused. Then she shot a glance at Malcolm. "But we didn't ruin our supper, honest."

He winked. "Thanks, honey. Nice save."

But Betsey seemed even more troubled now. She kept her voice light, however. "And did you have fun?"

"Yes!" Marguerite said. "Nana might let us have a slumber party with Gramps and her. Want to come, Mommy?"

Both women cast him startled looks.

Malcolm turned his palms upward. "Hey, I'm only the driver. I just now heard about this plan."

Betsey frowned. "Girls, Gramps can't go to a slumber party at Nana's house. And we'll just have to see what her plans are. Maybe now is not a good time."

They both groaned and began to plead about how much fun it would be.

Vanessa stood up first. "Please excuse me. It's been a hard day. I think I'll lie down for a few minutes."

"Can I get you anything?" Malcolm asked.

She shook her head. "Not at the moment. I just want to rest and hope my stomach will settle."

"Let me see them out, and I'll be right there."

"There's nothing you can do, Malcolm." But she might as well be saying the rest of it out loud. The words hovered in the air between them.

Nothing, except let me take care of this.

Malcolm exhaled sharply, drained by the weight of too many complications. His grace period was half-gone, and he hadn't yet convinced her.

"Daddy—"

He turned toward Betsey, noting the confusion on her face. "Bets—"

"Girls, go on out to the front yard and wait for me. I need to talk to Gramps a minute."

"Give me a hug, you gorgeous things." He knelt and opened his arms.

Both girls raced toward him and covered his face with kisses. "Thank you, Gramps. I love you."

"I love you, too, both of you. You be good now, and eat your supper so I don't get into too much trouble with your mother, okay?"

They giggled, then raced outside.

Betsey followed them but stopped at the front door and glanced toward the bedroom. "Perhaps we should talk on the porch."

Malcolm felt as though he'd been called to the principal's office. He closed the door behind them, prepared for her disapproval.

But she surprised him. "Oh, Daddy." She rose

to her toes and gave him a quick hug. "I'm so sorry."

When she stepped back, he could see tears in her eyes. He was shocked…and more than a little grateful. "Why, Bets?"

"She doesn't want the baby, does she? And you don't love her, at least not the way you loved Mother. But you adore children. This must be so hard for you."

He was stunned by how much she understood. "Did she tell you she didn't want it?"

"She didn't have to. What are you going to do?"

He shrugged. "I wish I knew."

"But you want it, don't you?"

He was grateful for the chance to talk about it. "Yeah. I do."

"You're a wonderful father. Grandfather, too, even when you're ruining their supper."

He clasped her small hand in his own, thinking how like her mother she could be when she wasn't feeling the bite of being the last child left. "What about you, Bets? You don't seem very happy to me lately. And it's not just Ria. I noticed it before she ever showed up. You and Peter having problems?"

She was her mother's child in many ways, tilting her chin upward though her eyes sparked with pain. "Marriage isn't always a cakewalk."

"Yeah." *But sometimes it's heaven and you still lose it.* "Anything I can do?"

She leaned into his side, sliding her arms around his waist, her voice strained. "No. I simply have to figure some things out."

He squeezed her shoulders and pressed a kiss to her hair. "After you get your life straightened out, want to see what you can do with mine?"

Her giggle was shaky. "I guess you offered to marry her."

"Yeah, not that it did any good. How did you guess?"

"Because you're the most honorable man in the world. You'd do the right thing, no matter what your heart wanted."

Her faith was touching, but he couldn't admire his track record. Now, more than ever, he questioned if he'd ever understood what the right thing was. But he simply rocked her in his arms and said, "Thank you."

"So what now?"

"I have no idea. She's determined to have an abortion."

"Oh, Daddy." Betsey pulled away, her expression troubled.

"It's her choice, I know. She's hit hardest, but—"

"It's your child, too."

"Yeah." On the lawn, his granddaughters waved

enthusiastically. He summoned a smile for them. "Maybe I'm too old to be raising another child."

"You'll never get old."

"I really believe I have a lot to give."

"Of course you do. And I'll help you."

Malcolm was deeply touched by her offer. She wasn't the mother he wanted for this baby, but his first choice wasn't available. "Thanks, sweetheart. That means a lot to me." He nodded toward the street. "The natives appear to be getting restless."

The girls had climbed into the car and plastered their faces against the glass, making streaks all over the inside.

Malcolm laughed. Betsey sighed, then chuckled. "Little monkeys."

"They're beautiful children, Bets." He squeezed her shoulders again. "You've done a great job with them." He looked down at her. "Are you mad that I took them to see Benjy?"

She hesitated, then shook her head. "He's not at fault. And he's probably had a rough life, hasn't he?" Her condemnation of her sister was plain on her features.

"So has his mother. We still don't know all that she's been through."

"She brought it on herself."

"Oh, Bets."

"I'm sorry. I can't stop thinking how different

everything would be if she hadn't—" She sighed.
"You and Mother would still be together."

"Maybe." He shrugged. "I'd like to believe so.
But maybe we weren't as golden as I thought. I
didn't—" He shrugged. "Never mind. Water under
the bridge." He glanced down at her again. "We
can't give up. I don't want to lose Vic—Ria again."

Betsey's jaw hardened. "She never brought you
anything but grief, Daddy."

He clasped his hands on her shoulders. "That's
not true. You have to remember the good times,
sweetheart. We'll find more of them."

Her eyes darkened. "She'll disappoint you
again. She'll hurt all of us." Defiance blazed. "I
can't forget what she's done."

"She made a terrible mistake, Bets, but your
mother and I let her down, too. You paid a price,
as well."

"It was a horrible time, Daddy. For you and
Mother, for me, for—"

"For her, as well," he reminded. "Families forgive, sweetheart. None of us is perfect. She's still
my daughter. Your sister. And she's been so alone."
He leaned forward. "Just give her a chance, Bets.
Please?"

"I'll try, Daddy. It's all I can promise." She
kissed him on the cheek. "Good night."

"Good night, Bets. I love you."

She turned back to him, this daughter who had spent her life attempting to please him. He wished he could convince her to cherish herself, instead.

"I love you, too. And if you—" She glanced at the door behind him. "If you need to talk, I'm always here."

"Thank you, sweetheart. I'm going to work this out somehow. You know me, the deal maker. I'll come up with something." Then he smiled, even though he didn't feel it. "But if you have any brilliant inspirations, speak up."

She seemed sad. "I will. I love you." She blew him a kiss and departed.

Long after she left, Malcolm stood on his front porch in the growing darkness and pondered what to say to the woman inside.

CHAPTER THIRTEEN

CLEO SHIFTED the bag to her left hand as she reached to unlock the shop. Before she could slip the key inside, Sandor jerked the door open.

"Don't you ever go home?" she muttered.

One eyebrow lifted. "The advantages of living nearby."

She peered closer. "You look terrible. What's happened?"

"Nothing."

"Sandor." She restrained him when he would have turned away. "You're disturbed."

He shrugged. "Restless night."

There was more to it, she was sure, but just then he stood aside and gestured toward the storeroom.

Then it hit her. "You've finished."

Sandor nodded.

"Let me see." She headed for the doorway of what had become his space.

When she reached the open door, Cleo stopped, heart in her throat. "Oh. Oh."

In the morning's golden light, the wood seemed to glow from within, the grain exploding with vitality, every curve alive. "I could swear she's breathing. It's exquisite. Oh, beyond that, I don't have the words. Lovely. Stunning. Sandor—"

"It is yours."

For a moment, what he said didn't sink in. Then she spun around, her eyes going wide. "You don't—I can't—" She was stammering. "It would be wrong for me to accept such a magnificent piece. You could sell it for so much. This will be the centerpiece of your show."

"You do not want it?"

"Of course I do, but—"

"If such a time comes, perhaps I would ask to borrow it, but it is yours, now and always."

As she started to protest, he shook his head. "There is more to tell you." He hesitated. "It is time, Cleo."

She sighed. "You're leaving."

He nodded. "It is…difficult. Being here has been a gift. I can never repay you for all you have done for me. Please do not refuse my poor gesture. It is not enough, but it is a beginning."

She tasted bittersweet sorrow, though she'd always known it would happen someday. She was losing a mainstay when so much of her life was a rough, rolling sea.

"Sandor, you can't believe you haven't given me back as much. All that you've done around here—" She gestured. "And you've been my friend when—" The thought of not having him here every day crashed down on her. "You've always been there when I needed one."

"That will not change. I am your friend, now and ever."

Then don't go, she wanted to beg. *Not now. Not yet.* But she didn't give voice to the plea. "I'm glad."

"So you will accept this?"

She turned to the sculpture again, and saw how elegant it was, yet so sensuous, alive with such grace and power it took her breath away. She knew she would never view it without imagining him in this room.

"All right." She turned back. "But I insist on loaning it to you when you have your first show. Which, I might add, should be sooner rather than later." Here she struggled for a smile. "Provided, of course, that I approve of the security arrangements."

He met her grin with his own. It was Sandor who had bullied her into updating the archaic security system on the shop, who had taken one look at her locks and muttered until he had replaced them all.

"You will call me when you need anything done around here." His eyes made it clear that it was not a question.

If her heart hurt a little that he was moving on, that he had so much life ahead of him that she'd already lived, Cleo didn't say it. She would endure, as she always had. "Just try refusing."

He lifted the bag she had dropped, gesturing for her to lead the way to the inside shop door. "How was your afternoon off? What did you and Benjy do?"

"Malcolm showed up with Elizabeth and Marguerite, wanting to take Benjy to the park. The kids begged me to go, too."

"And did you?"

Then Cleo was off and running, chattering about the things the children did, how they'd first circled each other like adversaries, then became a pack of rolling puppies. "And now we have plans for a slumber party. The kids want Malcolm to attend."

Sandor studied her. "And do you wish it, as well?"

"Of course not. They're too young to understand that it's impossible."

"Poor Colin. I begin to see the problem."

Cleo stared at him. "What do you mean?"

"His age is not the only strike against him. I hear it in your voice. You are still in love with Malcolm."

"That's ridiculous. We're divorced, Sandor."

"Since when does the heart pay attention to a piece of paper?"

"He has someone else now. He lives with her."

"He is spending a lot of time at your house lately."

"That's for Benjy." Cleo sniffed.

"If you wish to believe that." All merriment vanished. "I do not want him to hurt you. He walked away from you once."

"Because I asked him to go, not that it's any of your business." She continued before he could respond. "It wouldn't work. Too much has happened. We've grown apart."

"You are afraid."

"I am not."

"He is not worth fighting for?"

"He's got a younger woman. She's beautiful—tall and blond."

"You are beautiful, and you could have a younger lover, too, but you do not accept him. How do you know Malcolm does not have his own longings for you? Living together signifies nothing."

"I don't intend to discuss it."

"If that is your wish." But his skepticism was obvious.

"It is."

The phone rang, and he said he had to go, anyway. He left, and she busied herself inside. To seek out Malcolm, see if he—

No. She couldn't. She wouldn't know how, even if she thought that he—

She remembered how he'd stared at her on Sunday. How he'd wanted to stay for dinner a few nights before.

And a tiny voice in her heart whispered, *Why not?*

"LOOK, GRAMPS, there's Nana!" Benjy shouted from the tree-house window that afternoon. "Nana, me and Gramps are fixing more stuff on the tree house. Come see!"

Malcolm stopped nailing and glanced out. Cleo waved and crossed the grass, her form as willowy as the girl he'd first loved.

"Where's your mother, Benjy?"

"She went to see Aunt Betsey to ask if Marguerite and Elizabeth could play."

Malcolm and Cleo traded startled glances, but just then Benjy hung so far out the window Malcolm had to grasp his shirt to keep him from tumbling. "Hey, sport. Hold on. Nana won't be very happy if you fall on your head."

Benjy was far too excited to care. "Here, Nana. Climb on up."

"Oh, sweetie, it's been a long time," Cleo protested.

Malcolm couldn't help grinning. "Try the back window, Snow."

She laughed. Actually blushed. Malcolm hadn't forgotten how vividly her fair skin stained with color. He waggled his eyebrows. "Where's your sporting blood?"

"Hush, Malcolm. We're grandparents, for heaven's sake."

But he saw the memories dance behind her eyes. She hadn't forgotten. He never would. If this tree house could talk…

"You're not *too* old, Nana," Benjy said earnestly. "And Gramps climbed it, so maybe you could."

"Well, if Gramps, ancient as he is, managed…" She laughed. "But I'm wearing a skirt."

Benjy turned for help.

"We won't peek, will we, sport?"

"Uh-uh." Benjy shook his head. "At what?"

"Never mind. Wait here." With a quick drop, Malcolm was on the ground beside her.

Her eyes were wide and green, her expression breathless, shy as a girl's.

He ached to kiss her. To have her in his arms again. In his life.

She touched his wrist, and it was all he could do not to sweep her up, bear her off to—

He glanced away from the vision she made, fighting himself. He didn't love Vanessa, but the baby…

Her expression dimmed. Shuttered. She stepped away.

"Snow, I—"

"Benjy, I only dropped by for a minute on my way back to the shop from the bank. I have to close up tonight. You and Gramps have fun."

"But Gramps has to leave, too, he said."

Cleo glanced toward Malcolm.

"I have to meet—I, uh, have a meeting." Vanessa had called and asked to talk, but he avoided mentioning her to Cleo. They'd settled on the coffee shop near Cleo's store, Vanessa's favorite.

"Auntie and Grammy will still be here, and I'll be back to tuck you in," she said, her expression making it clear she knew exactly who he'd be joining.

"I want Gramps to do it."

"Sweetheart, Gramps doesn't live here. He has to go home to Vanessa."

Benjy's lower lip trembled. "I don't like Vanessa."

"But Gramps does." Her voice turned cool, her green eyes shadowed.

She'd understand if she heard the whole story, but it would hurt her so much. He had no idea what to do. "Snow—"

She ignored him. Hugged Benjy and slipped away.

"What's wrong with Nana, Gramps?"

What had he seen in her eyes? Hurt, yes. But… longing? Was it possible that after all these years—

"You'll be at the slumber party, right, Gramps?

Vanessa doesn't need you—*we* do. Me and Elizabeth and Marguerite. And Nana and Mom. We need you more."

Do you, Cleo? Do you want me as much as I'm beginning to realize I want you?

And, God help us, what do we do about it now?

CHAPTER FOURTEEN

SANDOR WAS SIZING UP the tools he'd have to pack, when he heard Betsey's raised voice from inside the shop, her normally pleasant tones tense and shrill.

Was she in trouble? He grabbed his sharpest chisel and made his way to the back door.

"Don't you ever get tired of running away?" Betsey challenged.

"Don't you ever get tired of passing judgment?" A woman's voice that sounded—

Familiar. His hand lowered. Betsey's sister. They had met on one of her visits to the shop. He'd quickly realized that the woman he'd found in trouble at Joe's had indeed been Cleo's troubled daughter about whom he'd heard so much.

He paused, uncomfortable listening but concerned. Would the infamous Ria harm her sibling? For Cleo's sake, he would bide a moment to be certain.

"It's so easy for you." Betsey's words dripped

with contempt. "Whip through like a hurricane, then leave everyone else to deal with the damage. You're the most selfish person I've ever met. You have no idea what you've done, do you?"

"It was six years ago, Betsey. I never meant for it to happen. Do I stay on trial forever?"

"David's dead. Mother and Daddy are divorced. You caused all of that."

"You don't think I hurt, too?" Ria's voice cracked. "I made a mistake—the biggest one of my whole screwed-up life. I'd sell my soul to bring him back, to return to the moment before we got into that car. I have no idea why I lived and he died—I wish I hadn't. I know you do, too. But he's still gone, and I can't figure out how to make any of it better."

"Go away," Betsey said. "Don't ever come back. We were doing fine until you showed up."

Ria's shoulders sank. "I can't do that to Benjy."

Betsey grabbed her sister's arm. "Leave him here. We'll take care of him."

Ria jerked away. "Abandon my child? With you? You hate his guts."

"I don't. He's not to blame."

"But I am—right, Bets? It's not enough that I pay every second inside my heart. I have to beg for forgiveness that you and Mother are never going to give. Only Daddy—"

Betsey cut in. "You let Daddy alone. He's got enough problems on his hands with Vanessa and the baby. Having you hanging around only makes things worse."

Sandor saw his same shock ripple over Ria's face. "Baby?"

Betsey's gaze darted away. "Forget I said anything."

"Daddy's going to have a child?"

"He isn't telling anyone yet. But the last thing he needs is your histrionics. He has a new family on the way."

Ria had gone ashen, visibly swaying on her feet. "But…but he loves Benjy and—"

"Mother and Aunt Cammie and Lola will look after Benjy." Betsey's voice softened. "He's innocent, and he deserves a better situation than you've provided him. Daddy and I will help. He'll have plenty of people to love him."

However much Sandor had wanted to dislike Cleo's eldest, pity moved him now. Betsey did not seem to be aware that she was eviscerating her sister with every word.

"I'm his mother," Ria whispered. "I love him."

"Enough to give him the life he deserves? Will you ever straighten out your own? And even if you did, how long do you expect Mother to support you?"

Sandor couldn't stand by and simply observe. He took one step into the office to tell Betsey to stop.

Just then, the bells at the front door jingled, and a customer walked inside.

"I'll be right with you," Betsey said. She turned back to her sister. "Vicky, I'm sorry. I shouldn't have told you about—" She glanced at the impatient customer. "Wait for me. I have to deal with this." She made her way to the front.

Ria didn't linger. She stumbled blindly into the room where Sandor stood.

He steadied her. "Sit." He closed the door to the shop.

She blinked, as if she'd imagined him. Dropped her head into her hands. "Go away."

"I think not," he said. "I will get you water."

Her mouth twisted in an imitation of a smile, even as misery filled her eyes. "You heard," she said dully.

He only nodded. "Here." He thrust a glass of water into her hands.

Mutiny marched across her face, but she drank. After a moment, she sank against the chair. "Is she right? Should I leave him here?"

"Betsey is not a bad person. She has borne a burden for all these years, trying to be the perfect daughter, to keep things tranquil. Your presence makes that difficult."

"So I just desert my child?"

"I did not say that. Only you can answer the question of where he is better off."

"It would make life so simple for everyone, wouldn't it? Daddy has his little nest, Betsey hers, Mother needs no one. But I—" She doubled over then, water sloshing in the glass gripped in one white-knuckled hand. "He's all I have. The only thing I've ever done right."

Pity moved him. "He is not all you have."

Her head jerked up. "What the hell do you know? Don't patronize me."

Compassion gave way to impatience. "You have the power to change everything, yet you fall into self-pity instead."

She lifted shocked eyes to his and rose. "I have no power. I'm the one who owes a debt that will never go away. I'll wait until my dying day for forgiveness that will never come."

He shrugged. "I, I, I. Me, me, me."

She slapped him.

He grabbed her shoulders. Shoved her away. "Go on, little girl. Run. Hide from growing up."

Her eyes were huge, burning holes in her face, testaments to dark rivers of pain and fury. "Go to hell," she spit.

She stalked out, wrapping herself in frayed remnants of pride and rebellion.

Sandor was about to make his way inside to check on Betsey, but after a few feet, he reversed his progress to watch Ria depart.

And when instead of going right, in the direction of Cleo's house, she turned left, on the path that would lead to Joe's Bar, he muttered a curse.

Then crossed to the phone, looked up a number and dialed.

In a few terse sentences, he secured the agreement of Hank, the owner, to keep an eye out for Ria and any trouble that might follow her. Then he headed for Betsey, wondering if Cleo would thank him for this night's work.

Two hours later, the call came.

MALCOLM PAUSED before he entered Lava Java, the coffee shop next to Cleo's store, and cast a glance to the side. For a second, he considered going over to see the window Ria had created, maybe visit with Betsey.

He could say it was to make certain they hadn't resorted to blows, and that would be part of his reason, all right.

In truth, Cleo was the lure. He wanted to peer into her eyes, find out if he'd imagined her response to him earlier. Was it possible that she missed him, too? Lay awake nights wishing to turn the clock back?

But what could he do about it, even so?

He yanked the door open. He was here to meet Vanessa, and time was running out. Cleo—and all his pent-up feelings about her—would have to wait.

But the second he entered, he heard Cleo's laughter, husky and low.

Like a heat-seeking missile, his gaze found her standing just inside the counter, face brightly lit with humor.

With a man who looked as though he'd like to devour her. A younger man, handsome and fit.

Who had his hands on her.

Before Malcolm could think, his own had closed into fists. He stepped toward them, seized by a primal urge to declare his territory. *She's mine, you pup. Get your hands off her.*

"Can I help you?" called a voice from behind the counter. "Sir?"

When he didn't answer, the man with Cleo turned his way. Surprise and something darker on the younger man's face.

Possession.

Malcolm barely stifled a growl.

Then Cleo saw him.

Pleasure blossomed, quickly chased by unease. Her cheeks flared with color. "Malcolm, what are you doing here?"

In an unconscious gesture of protection, she placed herself in front of the younger man.

Jealousy threw a poison cloud over Malcolm's good sense. He moved forward.

After a shocked instant, Cleo recovered and crossed to him. She laid one hand on his arm as if to settle him. "Is something wrong? Didn't you have a meeting?"

The younger man approached. "Cleo, are you all right?"

Malcolm tensed again.

Cleo's slender fingers squeezed. "Malcolm?"

He still wanted to know who the hell this guy thought he was. "Introduce us," he said to Cleo, but never took his gaze from hers.

Nor she from his. "Who?" Her eyes widened. "Oh."

Before she could comply, Vanessa walked through the front door.

And stopped flat, examining their odd tableau. "Malcolm?"

He bit back the urge to swear. Felt Cleo stiffen.

When her mouth twitched instead of tightening, his annoyance fled in the face of her irresistible mischief. A flicker of her highly developed sense of the ridiculous seemed to be speaking to him through her eyes. *How did we get into this predicament?* it said. He relinquished his fury and grinned at her, shrugging as though to say *What can you do?*

Cleo burst out laughing then, and Malcolm joined her.

And for a golden moment, they were a couple again, sharing a private joke. United against the world.

"Excuse me. I seem to have walked in at the punch line," Vanessa said. She got a good look at Cleo and faltered for only an instant before putting out her hand. "You must be Malcolm's ex. I'm Vanessa Wainwright."

Cleo removed hers from Malcolm's arm to exchange greetings. "This is Colin Spencer." With effort, she smothered her giggles, but her eyes still danced.

Malcolm couldn't stop staring at her.

"I'm delighted to meet you, Colin," Vanessa remarked as though the two of them weren't lunatics. "Best coffee in town, pastries to die for and fabulous decor to boot."

"Thanks," Cleo's admirer said. "We won a design award for it." He cast a glance at Malcolm. "Would you two like a table?"

Oh, you'd like to get rid of me, wouldn't you? Malcolm managed to drag his attention from Cleo but didn't respond.

Vanessa did. "That would be lovely." She did

her model's glide toward the counter. "I'll order. I know your tastes and what's good here."

Malcolm didn't budge.

The pup glared.

Finally, Malcolm gave the place a once-over. Easy to see why Vanessa favored it, all Scandinavian woods and metal, sleek and spare. Modern and merciless.

Just like his condo, now that he thought about it.

Much the same as his existence.

With Cleo, his world had exploded in color, hot reds, rich greens, ocean-deep blues. Cleo was tactile, so every piece of furniture had to appeal not only to the eye but to the skin and the skeleton. She was as likely to mix nubby cotton with satin, velvet with leather. Silk with corduroy. You sank into Cleo's chairs and sofas; found warmth and comfort in her kitchen. Bliss in her bed.

Life, and surprises, everywhere.

At last, Cleo stirred beside him. "I'd better finish my paperwork."

Malcolm glanced at Vanessa, then back at her, wishing he could offer a better alternative. "No pyrotechnics at the shop?"

Cleo shrugged. "Haven't been there yet. Dragging my feet, actually. The place is still standing, though. A hopeful sign, I choose to believe."

"Want me to go with you?"

She cast a grateful smile at him, then over to Vanessa. "No. I'll deal with it." A rueful shrug. "My turn, I think."

The atmosphere grew thick. Intimate with all they shared, past and present.

The puppy interrupted. "Before you leave, babe, I have something for you in the back."

Babe. Malcolm narrowed his eyes. He didn't like this guy's tone. Or his age. Or his looks.

Or the fact that he's in love with my wife.

Damn it. He had no rights here. She was a free agent.

But Malcolm's collar suddenly felt too tight.

"All right," Cleo answered softly. "See you later, Malcolm." She approached the younger man, whose face brightened with such naked hope that Malcolm could barely stand to watch.

And when that man slipped his arm around Cleo's waist and drew her toward the back…

Malcolm ground his teeth. Shoved away from the table, dodging the feelings crowding his chest. He knew he would do something stupid if he didn't leave this minute.

But Vanessa was headed his way with cups in her hands and serious intent on her face.

Malcolm stared at Cleo, watched her go. Couldn't seem to make his limbs cooperate. Drag his heart up from the floor. Gather his wits.

Until Cleo leaned into the younger man's side.

Then, from somewhere, Malcolm managed enough pride and spirit to sit down.

And lock his foolish heart back into its cage.

IT WAS STILL EARLY, but the whole house was asleep around Cleo. When she'd arrived at the shop, Betsey had been shaken but closemouthed about her encounter with her sister. Ria had already been gone.

She hadn't returned home for dinner or to put Benjy to bed, which wasn't like her. No matter her other shortcomings, Cleo couldn't fault Ria's devotion to her child.

So Cleo was worried. Hardly the first time.

She'd called Sandor to see if he knew anything but hadn't found him, either.

Aunt Cammie and Lola had conspired with her to entertain Benjy, and she was grateful that he'd adapted so well to being here that he'd easily accepted her made-up story about his mother working late at the shop on another design project.

Cleo had put Benjy to bed and read him a story, then tried to escape her own thoughts in a book. She'd lost the battle and climbed from bed to sit on the sunporch, wrapped in a quilt, where she and Malcolm had spent so many hours together.

Tonight, for intoxicating moments, she had felt

close to Malcolm. Sharing a private joke was seductive in its own way.

Vanessa and Colin could have been speaking Greek, in that span of time, for all the impact they'd had on Cleo and Malcolm. The world beyond them receded to a fringe. She smiled, thinking of the euphoria, the fun of having her own mischief reflected in Malcolm's sparkling eyes.

But Malcolm was not hers, as she'd been so quickly reminded. Vanessa had first claim now. She was his classic type, tall and cool blond glory.

And Colin. Poor Colin. He was a sliver moon hanging next to the sun. All she'd been able to see was Malcolm.

Just then, Cleo heard a vehicle stop in front of her house.

A door shut. Voices murmured on the sidewalk, heading her way. Cleo crossed the hall to Ria's room, and looked down at the lawn.

Shock froze her in place.

Sandor and Ria, heads close together, voices soft but frames taut and wary. Then he brushed her hair with his hand, the way he sometimes comforted Cleo. Cleo felt it like a knife stab to the gut.

Ria made her way toward the door with unsteady gait, and Cleo realized her daughter was drunk. Sandor watched her progress until the front door closed. He waited a little longer, then left.

Sandor would never have taken her drinking.

It had to be Ria's fault.

Cleo stood in her daughter's room in the darkness and waited. Pulled her unraveling composure around her like a threadbare cloak.

Unsteady steps climbed the stairs, entered the bathroom. After a few minutes, Ria came out. She entered the room without turning on the light.

Cleo switched on the lamp.

Ria jumped.

She was a wreck. "What are you doing to him?" Fury had Cleo by the throat. "He's a good man, Ria. A kind one. If you have to play your games, do so with someone else."

The girl who had appeared utterly defeated now hissed like a cat. "You're the only one who gets a boy toy, Mother?"

"Don't talk to me like that."

"At first I suspected that it was Sandor, but it's the coffee-shop hunk, right? He's years younger than you, Mother. Aren't you embarrassed? At least you can't get knocked up like Vanessa."

Cleo would swear her heart stopped. "What?"

Ria's focus darted to the side. "Nothing."

"No—tell me what you said."

"I didn't—" Ria hunched her shoulders.

"Vanessa is pregnant?" Dear God. And she'd actually fantasized—

"I—listen, Mother, I could be wrong. Betsey was mad and she threw it in my face. But maybe—"

"Betsey knows, too?" She'd humiliated herself. Malcolm had a young woman and now a baby on the way. A baby Cleo couldn't give him. A child to replace—

Cleo thought she might be sick. How could he? Tonight he'd—

"Mother, I—I'm sorry. I shouldn't have told you. I just—" Ria looked about eight years old and ready to cry.

But Cleo couldn't deal with Ria now. Not when she'd just seen her world fracture.

She walked to the door without registering a single step.

"Daddy loves you. I'm sure he does."

Ria could have said *I hate you* and hurt her less. But Cleo didn't have the words to explain that or anything else.

"It doesn't matter. Nothing…matters." Cleo drew herself up carefully so that she wouldn't fall to the ground, fragments of her heart scattered like a china teapot dropped on a tile floor.

What an idiot she'd been to be so tempted by him. To read into his reactions that their old attraction held power still.

They were divorced. Malcolm had every right

to a new family, another child. He'd made no promises. She'd leaped to the wrong conclusions.

How pathetic she must have seemed, all but leaning into him to be kissed this afternoon. Lost in his gaze tonight.

She had to get away. To think. "I need to be in the shop early. Good night."

"Mother—"

Cleo closed the door and made her way stiffly across the hall and out to her sunporch, then crawled back into the quilt.

There would be no sleep for her. Not this night. Maybe not for many more.

But the sun would come up. It always had.

And she would go on. She always did.

CHAPTER FIFTEEN

THE NEXT EVENING Malcolm approached the place
that was once his home as nervous as a kid arriving for a first date. He wiped his palms against his
jeans, then curled his fingers to knock.

Everything had gone south last night after Cleo
had departed with the pup. He still had no clue
what Vanessa had wanted to talk about, because
she'd clammed up. Returned to the office and
hadn't been home all night.

He hadn't tried to reach her, either. He'd spent
long, restless hours staring out at the hills, at the
carpet of city lights. Puzzling over his reactions.
Wondering how he'd deluded himself for five
years that he was over Cleo.

Life with her had been rich. Full. They'd been
not only lovers but best of friends. She'd believed in him, encouraged him, listened. Debated
problems—his, hers or theirs—shared every important event of his existence. Made him who
he was.

Loved him. Sheltered him. Given him babies and laughter.

He hoped he'd done half as much for her.

They'd been a team. Once, for so many good years, they'd been golden.

They could be that way again. And with her clever mind and compassionate heart, maybe she could help him figure out what to say to Vanessa to turn the tide. Some fair solution for Vanessa that would protect the baby, too.

Vanessa wasn't willing to be a mother—fine. He could raise the child himself. And maybe, with time, Cleo and he might—

He whirled from Cleo's door and looked out at the street. Was he actually crazy enough to even think it? Could he honestly ask?

But he wasn't a man to lie to himself. In the long hours of darkness, he'd seen the truth. Sure, he could make a good life for the child without Cleo. But he craved to have Cleo, too.

And he thought she might want him.

He dreamed of giving them both what they'd longed for—another chance. Benjy was Ria's, but this child could be his and Cleo's. Her heart held more than enough love for a baby she had not borne.

He shook his head and faced the door again, amazed at himself. Wondering if she'd slap him or laugh.

Or maybe, just maybe…say yes.

He was scared but oh, so alive. Taking a chance. He'd never liked life more than when he was skating on the edge, daring what couldn't be done.

He'd been on this earth enough years not to kid himself that this wouldn't be damn near impossible to pull off, but his back was against the wall. Vanessa's deadline expired in two more days, and he couldn't surrender without a fight. Somehow, he had to divine the magic solution for her—and the baby.

He'd never find a better partner in a fight than his Cleo. Cleopatra Felice Formby Channing, who looked like Vivien Leigh and had every bit the grit of Scarlett O'Hara.

So here he was, hat in hand, about to ask for her help, insane as such a course might be. Hoping the love that had never truly died in him was still alive in her, somewhere in the ashes of a marriage that they should have fought harder to save.

His hand trembled slightly as he knocked on the door.

"Gramps! Gramps is here!"

Malcolm smiled, hearing what sounded like the thundering hooves of a herd. Remembering many other slumber parties where he and Cleo had prayed to survive the night.

He was still grinning when Benjy opened the

door, jumping up and down. "Hey, sport." Malcolm caught the boy in his arms and lifted him high over his head, then settled him on his shoulders.

"Gramps, me next," Marguerite pleaded.

He gave her a turn, Marguerite as noisy as Benjy. Then Elizabeth slipped to his side and clasped his hand. He swept her up in his arms. "And how's my princess?"

Elizabeth's green eyes sparkled as he spun a slow circle. When he finally stopped, she threw her arms around his neck, giggling. "I'm dizzy, Gramps."

"Me, too." He pressed his lips to her forehead. They grinned like conspirators.

She looked past his shoulder. "Gramps is making me dizzy, Nana."

His heart gave one quick stutter. Malcolm wheeled to face Cleo, both eager and nervous. Wishing they were alone.

But the woman he'd hoped to see was nowhere to be found. This one smiled brightly, but it was all an act he'd witnessed before, when Cleo didn't trust…or when she was hurting.

She wore composure like armor when she felt most fragile, but he'd hoped never to find the shields raised against him again.

He frowned, glancing at the kids. "You all right, Snow?" Then he spoke to them, but kept his eyes on Cleo. "Kids, let me talk to Nana alone for a minute."

Her gaze skittered everywhere but at him. "Oh, no, that's not necessary," she said quickly. "The grill is almost ready."

"We're cooking hot dogs outside, Gramps," Benjy chattered. "And later, Nana says we can make these things called S'mores."

"You know, with marshmallows toasted over the fire?" Elizabeth demonstrated her superior knowledge.

Malcolm smiled at them, setting his grand-daughter on her feet. "Sure. That'll be great." But his mind was on Cleo and uncovering what had happened to her.

"Good," she said briskly. "Ria is outside, straightening coat hangers. Perhaps you could assist her. Marguerite, go wash your hands, since you've been petting Tyrone. Benjy and Elizabeth, come help me carry things out." The woman whose organizational skills could probably have created the world in one day less than God, giving them all marching orders.

Malcolm touched her shoulder as the kids brushed past them. "Cleo, we have to talk."

She didn't turn back. "I can't imagine why. If you'll excuse me, Malcolm, I'd better make sure no one drops anything. Thank you for helping Ria."

And just like that, she walked away. Malcolm rested his hands on his hips and exhaled. This Cleo, the one who could make you invisible if she didn't want to deal with you, wasn't his favorite.

But he had the home-court advantage. He understood something that most people didn't. When she got cold, she was hurt. The colder the shoulder, the deeper the ache.

It only made him want her more, to pull her into his arms and shield her from harm. Soothe away the hurt. Guard her heart.

Cleo had never really needed him to do any of that. She'd coped with everything life had ever thrown at her.

But it didn't make him quit wishing to be her champion anyway. Even though he'd failed to protect her from the one who'd hurt her most.

Himself.

And then it hit him.

The baby. Betsey must have told her about the baby.

Hell. Not that there was any good time for her to find out, but he'd intended to be the one to tell her.

That explained everything, though. How she held herself so stiffly, why she wouldn't meet his eyes.

His high hopes crumbled to dust. Malcolm saw himself for the fool he was. He'd convinced himself that he could woo her again, draw her to his cause. That she would care about what had become so important to him and view it as a gift, too.

She *did* have plenty of love inside her to give a child who was not her own; he was certain. But hadn't she been through turmoil enough? Everyone else was dropping into her life—Lola and Cammie, Ria, Benjy. How many causes could one small woman take on?

Malcolm dragged both hands through his hair, then dropped them to his side and confronted the hard facts.

He wanted Cleo. Loved her still.

But love didn't always mean that you could have your heart's desire. He'd wished for Cleo and the baby both.

But maybe he could have only one. That baby hadn't asked to be created.

"Gramps." Benjy raced into the room, plastic bag of hot dog buns swinging from his hand. "Come on. Mom could use your help with the coat hangers."

The small hand tugged at his own. He had responsibilities greater than his own longings. "Okay," he said, dredging up a smile. "Let's go."

When they reached the deck, Ria glanced up at him, then her gaze skittered away.

"Hi, sweetheart." He moved to her side and clasped her shoulders, brushing a kiss across her hair.

"Hi, Daddy." But she didn't look up, concentrating fiercely on straightening the coat hanger in her hand.

Malcolm narrowed his eyes. "You all right?" he whispered.

A quick nod, but still she didn't make eye contact.

Suddenly, he realized who, instead of Betsey, might have told Cleo.

Oh, man. As if she and Cleo didn't have enough problems.

Malcolm plucked the coat hanger from her hands and drew her a few short paces away. Out of the hearing of the others, he spoke softly. "What's wrong?"

She shook her head and studied the boards on the deck. "Nothing."

He tilted her chin upward. "It doesn't seem like nothing." He kept his voice carefully neutral. "You know. About the baby. Am I right?"

She nodded, eyes closed.

"Your mother does, too?"

She glanced up, misery darkening her eyes. "Oh, Daddy, I'm so sorry. I didn't mean to tell her. I was hurt and angry and—" She sighed and pulled away. "There's no excuse. All I ever do is hurt people." Before he could speak, she lifted her gaze. "Mother loves you. I know she does. You still love her, too, don't you?"

He shrugged. "If I did, it wouldn't change anything."

He ached for his daughter's misery. And her words kept repeating in his brain: *Mother loves you. I know she does.*

Benjy called out, "Mom, come on. We're ready to roast the hot dogs. Gramps, I want you with me."

Ria started to turn and then stopped. "She's upset, but don't give up now. There's got to be a way." She ducked her head. "And I'm sorry I made things worse. I don't expect you to forgive me."

"Ria—"

But she left his side too quickly for him to comfort her.

Malcolm pasted on a smile he didn't feel and joined the group.

SOMEHOW they made it through the evening, partly thanks to Lola. She took center stage from the three adults, who were struggling, and entertained the children until the adults could draw on their masks.

Malcolm gave more horseback rides than his aching knees would have preferred. Cleo wiped sticky fingers and faces coated with chocolate and marshmallow debris. Ria held Benjy on her lap as often as he'd let her, quietly observing her nieces but never venturing closer.

And eventually, the three children were tucked

in bed after Cleo had read them two stories. Lola and Cammie had long since retired, and Ria sought her room.

Only Malcolm and Cleo were left. He helped her straighten the ravaged living room, picking up scarlet cushions he didn't recognize, placing them on a sofa he'd never bought. All around him, the room that had once been so familiar whispered to his heart. Just enough touches of their shared past remained to make him remember more than was wise. Every memory drove the sense of loss deeper.

And the woman who was the soul of those recollections held herself carefully apart, a polite stranger at best.

He should leave, but she might never let him come back. There were things that must be said. He started with humor. "Thank God they're not in junior high. We'd never have survived."

Cleo glanced up, surprised enough to smile. "Please. It doesn't bear thinking." For a moment, their eyes met, amusement sparking between them.

Malcolm took heart. "Do you remember David's tenth birthday when he had ten boys over to spend the night?"

Cleo shuddered. "Don't. You'll give me nightmares."

But they both laughed, recalling waking up and

finding eleven boys up on their roof. Praying every second until Malcolm got them all down safely.

Then the laughter died, but its echo remained. Both went still, unable to look away.

"Snow, I wanted to be the one to tell you, but I didn't know how. I—the baby—"

She held up a hand, all traces of laughter gone. "You don't owe me an explanation. You have your own life now. There's Vanessa, and soon, a child." She swallowed visibly. "I'm…glad for you, Malcolm." The mask slid over her features again, her eyes too bright. "I hope you'll be very happy." She began rearranging the cushions she'd just straightened.

"Cleo, look at me."

She stopped fussing, but she didn't face him.

He grasped her shoulders.

Cleo jerked away. "Don't. You should go, Malcolm. *Now.*"

Maybe she was right. Perhaps that was smart. But damn it, he wasn't leaving until they'd talked this out.

"Not yet. You don't understand."

Her eyes narrowed. "You have no business here. Not anymore."

"I don't love Vanessa. I love you."

Her mouth dropped open.

Then she shoved at his chest, hard. "You bastard. How can you say that to me? How dare you, Malcolm?" Angry tears glistened. She pushed at him again, but this time he seized her hands.

"I don't blame you. I can guess what you're thinking, but you're wrong. Vanessa doesn't want this baby. She doesn't love me, and I don't love her." Cleo struggled to pull away and he gripped her hands. "Damn it, Cleo, listen to me. I need your help."

She trembled in his grasp. "Let me go, Malcolm."

"If I do, will you stay? Hear me out?"

Her chest heaved in outrage, her chin jutting, her eyes giving him that go-to-hell stare no one else did half so well.

Malcolm swore under his breath. Their arguments had always led to passion of another sort, and right now, his twice-damned body was remembering.

Hell. Right here, in the middle of the biggest screwup of his life, he craved this woman who would just as soon unman him for good.

"Stop squirming. You can't have forgotten how our fights always ended."

Cleo's voice was almost a growl. "Don't you even consider it."

But he could see memory flare.

It was all he could do to let her go. "Don't you think I realize how absurd this is? Please, Cleo. I won't touch you again. I just—" He raked his fingers through his hair. "I need you, as my friend. As the person who knows me best."

He turned up one hand. "I'm aware that I don't deserve your compassion. I let you down in the worst way anyone who claimed to love someone ever could. I had no idea how to get us past the pain, but I should have been able to figure it out."

Her eyes softened slightly. "You didn't do it by yourself, Malcolm. It takes two people to give up on a marriage. I let my grief become more important than any of you. And I'm the one who asked you to go."

"I told myself you'd be better off without me. All we did was blame each other. The wounds wouldn't heal because we didn't talk, and when we attempted it, we kept ripping them open."

"I don't know where the blame belongs. We tried with Ria. So hard. It just—maybe there was never any way for us to reach her." Her green eyes searched his. "And perhaps it was no one's fault. Just a terrible, cruel twist of fate."

She stood there, so small and brave. He wanted to put his arms around her more than anything on this earth. He flexed one hand, longing to touch.

But he'd already hurt her again without meaning it. Just when he was beginning to understand what he desired most, fate had stepped in with other plans for him.

His hand settled back at his side. "I'm in a hell of a mess, Snow."

Cleo's head tilted. "What do you mean?"

"Vanessa wants an abortion. Day after tomorrow is my deadline for figuring out an answer we can both live with. She never cared to have children, and she doesn't feel that she can interrupt her career right now, even if she did."

He laughed without mirth. "Pretty ironic. Remember me, the staunch defender of women's rights? Well, I'd have sworn I'd uphold any woman's privilege to decide for herself. I always have." He lifted his gaze to hers. "But guess what? When it's my child in question—suddenly, all my principles fly out the window."

"Of course you feel that way. You love children. You'll be a wonderful father, just as before."

Her generosity moved him to open up more. "I—it feels like a second chance, Cleo. A new child to—"

Her eyes darkened. "You can't replace David."

Fury rose. "Don't you think I realize that?" He began to pace. "But I've been haunted for years over all I wish I'd done, the things I should have said. And not just with David. With the girls." He turned. "With you."

She ignored his last words. "You can't undo the past, Malcolm. And every parent has regrets." Her own were clear in her tone. "Even with a new child, you'll make mistakes. You and Vanessa will struggle, just as we did."

"Vanessa won't be a part of this. She's already made that clear. I just have to come up with some way to convince her to bring the baby to term." He shook his head and exhaled. "I sound like a fool now. Wait till you hear my other idea."

Cleo frowned faintly. "What?"

He steeled himself. Might as well go for broke. "From the moment I learned of the child's existence, all I could think was what a great mother you are, how lucky this baby would be to have one like you."

For a second, she didn't understand.

Then she did. Her mouth made an O. Her eyes went wide in shock. "Malcolm, you can't possibly suggest—" Sparks erupted. "Unbelievable. You arrogant, selfish—that's the most—" She paused for breath, chest heaving.

"I understand. I do, I swear." His shoulders sagged. "It's out of the question. Not even fair to ask." He captured her gaze, owing her honesty. "But I'd be lying if I said I didn't wish for it, Snow, because it's true. You have more love in one finger than Vanessa has in her whole body. You'd never punish a child for not being your own flesh."

Cleo sat down heavily. "I have no clue what to say."

"How about 'You're a goddamn fool, Malcolm Channing, and get the hell out of my house.' It's the only smart response."

He went down on one knee in front of her, reaching for her hand. It was ice-cold. "And I wouldn't blame you. But you know me. Nothing ventured, nothing gained. You'd be the best thing that ever happened to this baby. We're one whale of a team."

He shook his head. "Damn, I am some kind of dreamer, aren't I? Always was. But before you throw me out of your house, Cleo, *please* help me figure out what I can say to Vanessa to make her understand what she's giving up. I don't deserve your consideration, but this baby does. I'm begging you. I'm all out of ideas."

Cleo studied him for a long moment. "We've had some bizarre conversations in our life together, Malcolm Channing, but I do believe this might take the cake." She passed her free hand over his hair, one stroke so light he could almost have imagined it.

But he hadn't. He smiled, ridiculously happy that she'd touched him of her own accord. "Ain't it the truth?" He sobered abruptly. "I really have no clue what to do. I can't find the magic words." The ache that had haunted him for days squeezed down hard.

Cleo's hand tightened on his, then she released him, her eyes gentle and sad. "If you're ever to convince that woman, you need to be spending time with her, not with me, Malcolm. Maybe you don't love her now, but that doesn't mean affection could never grow between you. No woman is interested in being a broodmare for a man who doesn't love her. You've got to try to make it work, for that baby's sake. Go back to her and tend whatever seeds of caring you have. Focus on what's good in her and build on that."

"But she's not the woman who holds my heart." Was this truly the end for them? No more second chances?

Silence swirled, smothered. Pain crowded the room.

Cleo's eyes were bleak. He was sure his were, too.

"Damn it, it's not fair." He gripped her hands, willing her to change her mind.

"Malcolm..." Head down, hunched over, she tried to withdraw, but he wouldn't turn loose.

One tear dropped on his fingers. Another.

"This is killing me, Snow. How am I supposed to let you go again?" he whispered.

A cry escaped her. She struggled against his hold. "Please. I can't—" The look in her eyes tore something deep inside him. "What we want doesn't matter. And who you love can change."

"You're wrong," he shouted. Shoved to his feet. "You're the only woman I've ever loved. Ever will. This can't be how it ends." He wanted to punch a fist into the wall.

"It's been over for a long time, Malcolm." Her voice shook. "What we had is gone."

"It's not, damn it. You didn't stop loving me, just as I never quit loving you." His pacing arrested in midstep. "Is it that guy, that…kid you were with? If he wasn't in the picture—" He stared at her in horror. "Are you in love with him, Snow?"

"No. He thinks he is, but—" She glanced away, then straight into his eyes, though the suffering he saw there nearly undid him. "He's not the issue. The child is all that counts, Malcolm. Not us. Not the past."

He started to grab her, to shake her. Force her to acknowledge that their love would never be gone. Couldn't die.

The violence of his emotions shocked him straight.

"Cleo." Her name on his lips was part prayer, part anguish.

She was right. A child's life was at stake. His longings couldn't weigh in the balance.

But God, it hurt. Like a cancer eating its way into his bones, the thought of losing Cleo forever, of being only kind strangers from now on, corroded all the hope within him. Nearly brought him to his knees.

Why had he been blind for so long? How could he have overlooked for a second that she was part of him forever, that he'd never be whole without her?

When she lifted her head, he could see his torment reflected in her agonized gaze. Everything in him called out to her, desperate to be one again.

"Snow." His voice was raw with yearning. "Could I hold you? Just once?" One more embrace that would have to last him for a lifetime.

Every day for as long as he lived, he would miss her. And he would have to see her again and again, aware each moment that they could never be together. The grinding ache had him reaching out to pull her into his body, to warm them both.

For a second, she softened against him.

Then, with a broken sob, Cleo stumbled away. Stuck out a palm to keep him back.

The rejection was a fist to his gut.

He couldn't help grasping for her again, but she staggered back. "No. Malcolm, *no.*" She wrapped her arms around herself and fought to hold herself rigid. "We'd only make it worse." Her voice barely stirred the air between them, but her eyes…oh, God, those eyes he had loved for so long. They told him just how much he'd lost.

He could ignore her. He was stronger, bigger. If

he could touch her, he could make her recant. That had always been true between them.

But he had hurt her too much already.

So instead, he fought with himself until he'd wrestled down the need. Cleared a throat that had closed up so tight he could barely breathe.

Then he dredged up the strength to do what was right, though he wasn't sure his legs would hold him.

"I'm sorry." His vision blurred as he headed for the front door.

Hand on the knob, he paused but didn't turn back. "I'd still like to see Benjy as often as possible, but I'll make sure you're not here."

He might have heard her whisper his name.

But he didn't wait to find out.

IT WAS NEARLY MORNING, and Cleo had no idea what had happened to the night.

Except that it was colder than usual, she thought.

But that might only be her heart. Still in her clothes, wrapped in an afghan topped by a quilt, she couldn't seem to stop shivering. Find any warmth.

She tried to understand what was different. In reality, she'd watched morning come only a matter of days ago, and Malcolm had been out of her life as much then as now.

She doubled over, legs drawn tight, arms wrapped around them to still the shaking.

You know, Cleo. You know.

A smattering of days before, she'd understood her life. Her place in the world.

Hadn't had her eyes opened. Believed Malcolm didn't love her.

Been certain she didn't want him.

Was there anything more cruel than discovering that the one true love of your life loved you back as deeply as ever—

Only to have to face that you would never be together again?

Oh, it wasn't that she didn't believe him that Vanessa and he weren't close. Or understand that these days, divorce was all too common, that Malcolm could leave Vanessa, share custody of the baby and come to her.

But Cleo had wrecked enough young lives. She could not live with herself if she damaged this baby's chance at happiness.

Cleo threw her head back against the chaise. From her throat was torn a sound caught between laughter and a sob, harsh and clawing. Ugly and… broken.

Because she was actually considering going to Vanessa and making Malcolm's case for him.

How could Vanessa live with him and not see

what kind of man he was? Strong, upright, compassionate to a fault. Honest and good. Kind. Caring.

And fun.

Oh, the fun they'd had together. She glanced at the shadowy profile of the tree house below, her mouth quirking in remembrance of heated kisses, of the feel of Malcolm's hair brushing her breasts, her midriff…her thighs.

Laughter strangled by the grip of overwhelming passion. Desire so hot she was sure normal women didn't experience it, or how would they ever get anything done?

A new memory surfaced. His hair tonight beneath her hand. The strands of silver mingling with mink-brown. But still thick.

Still beloved.

And off-limits.

Cleo bowed her head. Sank to the cushions. Curled against the pain.

Tears leaked beneath her eyelids, hot, stinging drops of grief and pain.

Over, it's over…he won't be mine ever again.

The birds began to chirp, small, hesitant nudges against the night.

Cleo gripped her hands inside her cocoon, nails digging into flesh.

And prayed to stop shaking. Cease feeling. Aching.

Recognizing that a small part of her had never truly given Malcolm up.

Wondering how on earth she ever would.

CHAPTER SIXTEEN

"SHE'S GONE."

Cleo stirred at Lola's voice. Groaned. Surprised that she'd fallen asleep at last, she tried to sit up. "What?"

"Ria. She's gone."

Cleo scrubbed at her face. "Already? Where?"

Lola huffed, settled beside her. Snapped her fingers. "I'm sorry, but you have to wake up, Cleopatra. Focus. Your daughter has disappeared."

"But—" Then it hit. "Oh, dear God, Benjy—" She struggled out of the covers and jumped from the chaise.

"He's still asleep."

Cleo frowned. "Then she'll be back. She'd never leave him."

Lola looked a thousand years old and brandished a slip of paper. "Read it for yourself."

"I don't understand."

"You will." Lola shoved the note at her. "I'm sorry, doll. This is my fault."

"Your fault?" Cleo echoed dully. "I'm the one she hates."

"Just read it, hon."

With foreboding, Cleo opened the paper. And saw her daughter's handwriting for the first time in years.

Mother

I can't pull this off. I can't be the good child you want. And I can't take care of Benjy the way he deserves, but I have no doubt you will. Betsey's right—you and Daddy will do it better, and the others will help you.

He'll miss me, and I'll never get over missing him. But I'll screw him up if I stay, just like I've destroyed everything else. For once in my life, I'm going to do the right thing. I heard you and Daddy last night, and I realize what I've cost you. I'm sorry, so sorry that I told you about the baby. I keep screwing up.

I'm running away again, and I know I've done that too often. But I'm leaving the best part of me behind. Let me give you a child to replace the one I cost you. You'll take better care of him than I ever could.

But please—don't let him ever believe I

don't love him. He is my heart. The only good thing I ever did.

                                    Victoria

Cleo pressed one hand against her mouth. "Oh, Ria. We were doing better. I thought we had a chance." She stared at her mother. "What have I done to her?"

Then she glanced at the words again. "What does she mean, Betsey was right?" She recalled her youngest daughter's pinched look after Ria had left the shop night before last. "Do you suppose Betsey told her to go and leave Benjy here?"

"Even if she did, Betsey didn't give the final push. I did."

Cleo had never seen her mother like this, drained and defeated. Lola always believed something better was just around the corner. Cleo sat back down and took her mother's hand. "You're Ria's favorite. You'd never harm her."

Moisture shimmered in Lola's eyes. "I didn't mean to."

"Tell me."

"Late last night, she came downstairs because she couldn't sleep. I was up watching TV. She just seemed to need company, so we talked. If I'd had any idea she was considering something like this, I'd have kept my big mouth shut." Lola gripped

Cleo's fingers. "I told her that I'd done the wrong thing, keeping you with me. That I'd been selfish instead of choosing what was best for you. I didn't marry a perfectly kind man because he didn't fit my image, and by refusing, I robbed you of the family you deserved. I was too busy dreaming my way to the top." Her eyes were old and tired. "I needed you, more than you ever needed me. I'll never be able to convey how much I regret that. And now look what I've done."

Cleo felt her mother's faint trembling. "You weren't selfish."

Lola laughed without mirth. "Doll, you're not the actress in the family. You can't lie worth a damn. You grew up in spite of me, not because I was a good mother."

"I always believed you loved me, in your own way."

"My own way won't win any prizes." Lola shook her head. "But that's the past. What are we going to do to find your child?"

Cleo's shoulders drooped for just a second before she straightened again. "You wake Aunt Cammie. Let's get coffee going and try to make the day as normal as possible. We'll tell Benjy—" Sweet heaven. What would they tell him? "We'll say that she—" What was right? He was too young to understand.

But what if they never located her? She was

older and wilier now, and she'd managed to stay hidden for six years.

But you gave up too easily then, Cleo.

It was true. Malcolm had kept searching, but she'd managed to bury her daughter's existence as deeply as she'd locked away her love for her husband. She'd fallen back into old habits, trusting no one, opening to no one.

Except Sandor, and him only a little.

Sandor. She stood suddenly. He'd been with Ria night before last. "Sandor might guess where's she's gone," Cleo said. "The police won't take a missing person's report yet, but we can talk to Betsey, as well. And find a private investigator. I wish we had more information about where Ria was during those years." With quick gestures, she folded the quilt and afghan, closing them up as she must put away last night. Nothing else mattered but caring for Benjy and finding her daughter.

She crossed the porch to enter her bedroom.

"What about Malcolm?"

Cleo stumbled against the threshold. "What about him?"

"He's her father, doll. He'd want to know."

I can't bear to see him again this soon.

But Lola was right. He'd been a better parent to Ria than she ever had.

"What happened between you two last night, honey?"

Cleo clutched the door frame. She didn't want to talk about it, but Lola would stay after her unless she understood why Cleo couldn't see him, so she took a deep breath and turned. "Malcolm and Vanessa are expecting a baby."

Lola was too much the romantic not to read between the lines. "Oh, sweetheart, I'm so sorry." She rose and drew Cleo into her arms. "But he still loves you. Any fool can see that."

The oddities never quit. The last time her mother had comforted Cleo, Cleo had been little older than Benjy.

Sorrow made strange bedfellows, but Cleo surprised herself by accepting Lola's embrace. "It doesn't matter." She couldn't let it.

Then she heard Benjy's voice in the hallway and stepped back. "We'll tell him that Ria did such a good job on the shop that she's gone to market in Dallas to get more supplies, and it will take a few days." Her gaze implored her mother. "Am I right that he's too young to be told the truth unless—" When was the last time she'd asked her mother for advice?

She wouldn't finish the sentence or voice her fear that they might never find Ria.

"I'm no expert at mothering," Lola reminded her, stroking one hand down her arm.

"I'm not, either," Cleo admitted.

"This will sound odd, coming from someone whose grasp on reality has never been that firm." Lola paused, and a trace of spirit sparkled in her eyes. "But perhaps as much of the truth as he can absorb is the best path. We could tell him that she loves him very much and that she thought he would enjoy a little vacation with us while she took one of her own because she's very tired and has been advised to rest."

"How can she do this to us?" Cleo cried. Heartache warred with a touch of anger. Why take the easy way out and not stay long enough to explain this to Benjy herself, instead of forcing Cleo to make agonizing choices?

And just how would you explain to one of yours that you were leaving them for their own good?

For that matter, how did you explain to Betsey why suddenly she had no father or siblings?

Let he who casts the first stone...

Ria had to be terrified right now, and heartsick to the bone. Despite her daughter's many mistakes, there was no doubt in Cleo's mind that Ria loved her child with everything in her.

She'd never have left him, otherwise.

"All right," she said. "And we'll tell him over

and over how much his mother loves him." She gave Lola a quick, awkward hug. "And we'll work night and day to find her, because she's wrong. He needs her most of all."

She started toward the hall to fetch Benjy, but halfway there, she halted. "Mother?" The forbidden appellation rose to her lips, surprising them both. "May I ask you a favor?"

For once, her mother didn't correct her. Instead, she smiled and blinked back tears. "Anything."

Cleo felt absurdly young and unsure. "Would you call Malcolm for me? I just—" *Can't.*

Lola nodded. "You got it, doll."

"GRAMPS!" Benjy was across the floor like a shot, leaping into Malcolm's arms.

Cleo had thought she had herself prepared to deal with Malcolm, but she realized she wasn't even close.

Was there anything that could melt a woman's heart faster than the sight of a strong man tenderly holding a small child?

And when that strong man's eyes opened and looked at you with his naked heart on display... She'd have to be a stone not to feel the earth shift beneath her feet.

Fortunately for her, Benjy immediately claimed

his grandfather's attention. No other concerns could come first.

"Gramps, my mom went on 'cation. She has to rest, that's what Nana said, but we'll do all kinds of fun stuff, and—" His precious little face crumpled, and he took a deep, shuddery breath. "And then she'll be back real soon. Right, Gramps? Nana says Mom will come home before we know it." His need for Malcolm's confirmation was palpable.

Malcolm cast Cleo a glance she couldn't interpret, but instantly shifted his attention back to the boy. "Your mother loves you with all her heart, Benjy. She'll return just as soon as she possibly can."

"But how long is 'soon,' Gramps?"

Cleo had forgotten a small child's fluid sense of time. Next week and next year were equally incomprehensible distinctions.

But Malcolm rose to the occasion, pasting a smile on his handsome face. "Well, there's ice cream soon and Christmas soon, and then there's bath time soon. Seems to me that bath time always comes quicker than Christmas, and ice cream's somewhere in between."

The threatening tears were lost as Benjy contemplated this puzzle.

"Your mom is supposed to rest up. Maybe we should say she'll be home Christmas soon because Christmas always feels far off, but when it arrives, it's really, really big fun. Having your mom home will be even better than Christmas, don't you agree?"

"Yeah." Benjy nodded enthusiastically, apparently as reassured by Malcolm's calm certainty as their children always had been. "So what will we do for our 'cation today? And can Tyrone come?"

All four adults in the room laughed in sheer relief. Other difficult moments would arise—bedtime, for one—but Cleo was reminded of some of the blessings of small children: they were flexible, and they took their cues from those around them. Remaining positive was key to getting Benjy through this.

Aunt Cammie stepped in then, recruiting Benjy to chaperone Tyrone and her on a walk. After hugs and kisses all around, soon Cleo, Malcolm and Lola were alone.

The atmosphere took a nosedive. If Lola hadn't been there, Cleo wasn't sure what she would do. Part of her yearned to assume Benjy's place in Malcolm's arms.

But nothing had changed since last night.

Not between Malcolm and Vanessa, anyway.

For Cleo…everything had.

Never had it been more critical for her to maintain her poise.

Never had she wanted to do so less. "Oh, God, Malcolm. What if something happens to her?"

"Would you care?"

She recoiled. "How can you ask me that?"

"I'm sorry. I'm still—" In his eyes she saw that his night had been miserable, as well. "Struggling to catch up. I just meant that she makes your life very difficult."

"She's tougher on herself."

As if she were a bright student who'd given the right answer, Malcolm nodded. "She strikes out at you because she doesn't believe she can ever measure up."

"To what?"

"To you. Who you are, what you demand."

"I don't—" But she did. She had. She'd expected Ria to understand how much better her childhood was than Cleo's had been. To pull herself together as Cleo always had.

In that instant, a memory surfaced, one she hadn't had in years. *Ladies' lunch.* Victoria, second grade, perhaps, in a green-and-white dress to match her own. So eager to go, so afraid Betsey would be included, that she bumped a table and nearly knocked over a lamp in her haste to leave.

Then off to eat tiny sandwiches and drink tea from terrifyingly thin cups. *We'll paint the town red, sweetheart.* Victoria had laughed. *All the buildings will be red, Mommy?*

Malcolm with a very disappointed Betsey kissing them both goodbye. *You're as beautiful as your mother,* he'd said. Victoria, blinking. *I don't think so, Daddy. Mommy's perfect.*

Cleo's shoulders sank as she remembered that earnest child who'd tried so hard—until the point came when she gave up. *Hardly perfect, honey.* She'd been the one who'd let Ria down, more than Ria had ever failed Cleo.

She was compelled to voice her deepest fear. "What if the note is a—" She couldn't say the word. "Malcolm, what if she hurts herself?" A cold finger of dread scraped its nail across her heart.

She would never forgive herself for losing another child.

Especially this one.

"I thought things were getting better, but I was kidding myself, wasn't I? I failed her in the worst way possible—me, who was ready to take him away from her, convinced I'm so much better—and she trusts me to nurture her child. How do I live with that, Malcolm? I drove her to this because I couldn't let go of my grief over David. Just as I pushed you away." She dropped her head and looked at the floor. "This is all on my shoulders."

"No, doll, it's not," Lola interjected. She seemed years older suddenly. "I bear a part in this, too."

"The time for recriminations is over, ladies. We must act. Even if we can't turn to the police because she left willingly, I'll call in some markers from people I know at the paper. We'll explore radio, TV, in addition to the private detective." He clasped Cleo's hand. "We'll find her, Snow. Don't assume for a minute we won't."

"At least the note doesn't sound as if she intends to harm herself, does it?" Cleo's eyes begged him.

Lola made a small, distressed sound.

He frowned. "What?"

She shook her head, glancing at Cleo.

"Oh, no." A ball of ice formed in the pit of her stomach. "Has she attempted it before? Tell me, Lola. Has she?"

Lola's eyes filled with tears. "She has scars on both wrists. She isn't aware that I saw them while she was asleep, but—"

"Dear God." Cleo gripped the counter as her knees went weak. They had to think fast. Find her faster.

"Where would she go? Who does she know?" Malcolm asked.

"She doesn't have any friends. She wouldn't go to Betsey," Cleo said.

"What about that Sandor guy?"

"I tried him earlier. What makes you consider him?"

"She mentioned him at the slumber party. Said he was a friend."

"I'm not sure I'd call him that." The vicious confrontation with Ria loomed large. "He brought her home. She was drunk."

"That bastard—"

"It wouldn't have been Sandor's fault, Malcolm. He's much more the knight-in-shining armor type. I intended to ask him about it the next day, but before I got a chance, she told me about—"

She could see that he understood instantly.

"She was sick at heart that she spilled it." Malcolm's jaw tightened. "Snow, I'm so sorry."

"It's not important now."

Malcolm's expression was part misery, part disbelief. But he didn't challenge her. "Phone him again. See where he found her."

She dialed Sandor's cell phone. "Sandor, thank goodness. I'm sorry to disturb you, but have you seen Ria?"

"What?"

"She's gone. We can't figure out where else to check."

"Perhaps she is only late."

"No, she took her things." Her voice trembled. "She left a note."

"Where is her son?"

"Still here. She wrote that he was better off without her. I'm afraid she—" Cleo swallowed hard. "Might hurt herself."

When he didn't respond, her heart sank. "You've seen the scars on her wrists, haven't you? Sandor, I'm terrified for her."

"Have you contacted the police?"

"They can't do anything yet. Malcolm is contacting private investigators."

"He is there with you?"

"Yes."

"Do you want me to come?"

Her breathing hitched. "Thank you for asking, but I'll be fine. Sandor, I need to know what happened the other night."

He didn't respond.

"Sandor?"

"Yes?" His tone was reluctant. Distracted.

She frowned. "I said I need to know what happened the other night. Where you found her."

"I am sorry to say that she was at Joe's Bar." His tone wasn't encouraging.

"I'm aware that she was drunk. Did she mention anything to you that might help us figure out where she's headed?"

"Cleo, I would rather not—"

She didn't let him finish. "It doesn't matter how

unpleasant the news is. We can't afford to overlook anything."

He exhaled. "I understand. This was not the first time I had found her there."

Cleo squeezed her eyes shut to block out Malcolm's worried expression. "Go on."

"Both times, she was having difficulties with... patrons."

"Sandor, stop protecting me. Exactly what was happening?"

"I was not sure it was her the first time. She was in the parking lot with a man who—" He paused. "I managed to intervene before it went too far, I believe."

"Dear God. What about the other night?"

"Suffice it to say that she brought her troubles upon herself. She was very drunk and miserable, and she took...risks. I got her out of there immediately."

"And?"

"We argued. I do not like what she does to you, though that night I understood her pain. She had had a fight with Betsey, and Betsey had told her that if she loved her child, she should leave and let you have him. Ria was distraught."

"Dear God." Malcolm wasn't going to stand still another minute, she could tell. "Hold on." Quickly she filled him in. Her anxiety was reflected on his face. "Where could she have gone, Sandor?"

"You might check David's grave."

"His…grave? But she doesn't—"

"She asked me to take her there, said that she had never seen it because she had been sedated until after the funeral."

Cleo clutched Malcolm's tense forearm. "How did she react?"

"She was terrified. She collapsed before she could make it all the way. I took her home then, but something about her manner made me believe she might return."

"Oh, sweet Lord," Cleo murmured. "Sandor, if you think of anything else—the slightest scrap that might help us, please call me."

"Shall I meet you there?"

"I—" *Yes. I could use a friend.* But she and Malcolm had to do this together, whatever else stood between them. "No. But thank you, Sandor."

She replaced the phone. "He thinks she might go to the cemetery. She wanted to see where David was buried, and so he showed her—" Tears threatened. She pressed a hand to her mouth. "He said she fainted before she ever got near."

She stared at Malcolm in horror. "What have I done?"

He snapped into action. "Lola, I'll keep you

posted. I've left my cell number with two private investigators."

Lola nodded and gave Cleo a quick hug. "Stop blaming yourself. You didn't do it alone. We all have parts to play. And don't worry about Benjy. Cammie and I will keep him occupied until you get back."

Malcolm grasped Cleo's hand and led her out the door.

He noted how she detached herself as soon as they were outside and stifled a protest, but he still walked beside her to open the car door as he always had.

Cleo seemed startled, as if having doors held for her was a forgotten luxury. "Thank you." Once seated, she clasped her hands carefully in her lap.

He rounded the hood. Her politeness made him want to slam a fist into the vehicle. He had to remind himself that critical parts of their situation had not changed, despite the nasty new curveball life had thrown them.

"Snow—Cleo," he corrected as he drove. "I know you don't want to be anywhere near me right now, but—" He paused, not sure what to say.

When she didn't respond, he cast her a quick look.

She was too pale. Too still.

Pity moved him to lay his hand over hers.

"We'll find her, I swear it. I won't give up, no matter how much it costs or how long it takes."

Still no answer.

He squeezed her fingers. "Stop blaming yourself."

A shudder ran through her. "Who else?" she asked in a haunted tone. "No good mother would ever have withheld herself from her child."

"You had reason." Not the least of which was Cleo's own childhood. She'd had no one to trust. To lean on. Though she'd wanted to love and be loved worse than anyone Malcolm had ever met, she was also more terrified of making herself vulnerable.

"Not good enough." She stared out the windshield as if she could force the miles to pass. "What if—" Her voice was barely a whisper. "What if we're too late?"

It was his own worst fear, and he had nothing to combat it for either of them. Ria was filled with self-loathing, he understood better now. If he'd known about those scars—

"We won't be." He sounded too harsh, but he needed to believe it as badly as Cleo did.

Cleo, however, had a greater store of experience with life's brutal realities. He could feel from her that she understood his bluster and the impotence of it.

So he said nothing else.
But he didn't let go.

ONLY THE WARMTH of Malcolm's hand kept Cleo from turning into a block of ice. Her heart was already frozen solid with fear. The miles to the cemetery were endless, yet she was terrified to arrive and find Ria not there.

As they drove through the gates, all her focus was fixed on the far side of the cemetery, wishing away the trees and curves blocking her view.

She wondered how often Malcolm came to this place. She still visited several times each year and never missed David's birthday, arriving in the hours just as dawn broke, the time of his birth. At first she'd visited on each anniversary of his death, but Sandor had helped her realize, two years ago, that she would never emerge from her grief if she didn't learn how to celebrate his life instead of battering her sanity against the futility of his death.

"Damn." Malcolm's grip went slack in hers.

They were near enough to tell that the grassy space held no visitors. Only the simple gray stone that marked their youngest child's final resting place.

Cleo wrapped her arms around her middle. Hope gasped for air as guilt's choke hold tightened.

Suddenly, Malcolm leaned forward against the

steering wheel. "Wait—when's the last time you were here?"

"What?"

"Did you bring flowers recently?"

"I don't understand—" She glanced at Malcolm, then at the grave finally in view.

Saw the bouquet. "Those aren't mine."

"Mine, either. Come on." He killed the engine and leaped out, pausing only long enough to help her emerge. His long strides ate up the ground, so he grabbed hold and pulled her with him.

With every step, Cleo prayed. *Please, oh, please—let us find a note, a clue—anything. I'll do it right this time—just give me another chance.*

They ran across the wet grass, hand in hand. Fell to their knees on either side of their son's grave.

"Daisies," she said. Once Ria's favorite flower, back in a distantly remembered past. "She was here, but—"

"Look." Malcolm pointed with a hand that wasn't quite steady, then unearthed a paper from beneath the blossoms.

David, it said on the envelope.

He glanced at Cleo. "This is private. She's lost so much. Do we have the right to read it?"

"I don't want to hurt her anymore, but we have to find her to help her."

Malcolm nodded. "I agree." He slit open the envelope, drew out the sheet inside. Scanned it quickly, and sagged. Proffered it to her.

David, I don't know how to make it up to anyone—Daddy or Mother or Betsey—and I can't bring you back, no matter how I wish I could take your place.

I tried to die once, but a friend saved me. I've thought about doing it again, but then I imagine how they'd feel, losing another one. About the kind of legacy I'd be leaving Benjy.

I have a son, Benjamin David, and he looks so much like you. He's good inside, just the way you were.

So I have to do what's right for him because he'd find out someday if I took the easy way out. It's bad enough that he'll learn everything I've done anyway. I'm so scared of how he'll feel.

Before he died, my friend Dog Boy made me promise to square things with Mother and Daddy and Betsey. I tried to tell him it wouldn't work, but you can't renege on a deathbed promise. Besides, he saved me when I first ran away and stuck with me when I got pregnant. If not for him, Benjy wouldn't be alive.

So I came back from California, but I was

right, and Dog Boy was wrong. Now I'm doing what Lola says she should have done for Mother, what Betsey told me was best for him, even though it feels like dying. I'm offering him a family who can provide the safety and security he deserves. I understand now just what I cost Daddy and Mother when my mistakes took their favorite child. Maybe by giving up mine to them, some of the pain I've brought will be healed.

Maybe someday, I can make something of myself and deserve Benjy again. If I do, I'll come back to see you, I promise.

I never knew why you loved me so much, Davey. I can only hope that wherever you are, you understand that I didn't deserve your love, but it meant everything to me.

Watch over my baby, please. Daddy and Mother and the others already love him, but everyone can use a guardian angel.

Ria

Devastated, Cleo looked up at Malcolm.

The tightness around his mouth eased. "She's not going to kill herself."

Guilt loosened its grip a fraction. "No." She closed her eyes. "Thank God."

"Come on, Snow." He helped her to her feet.

They paused then, side by side, in front of their son's gravestone.

"Watch over her, too, will you, sweetie?" Cleo asked, brushing her fingers over the stone. "She needs love worse than any of us."

Malcolm bent and placed his hand beside hers. "We love you, son. We'll bring her back as soon as we find her."

Cleo glanced up at him. "Will we?"

"You better believe it. We have two clues: California, and a guy's name. That's more than we had before." He slipped one arm around her shoulders. "Now, let's go take care of her boy."

THE DAY PASSED IN A BLUR. By tacit agreement, both stayed at the house, handling business concerns by phone. A distraught Betsey had been more than willing to handle an extra day at the shop, bringing the little girls to play with Benjy, which made for a perfect distraction. Either Cleo or Malcolm was always with Benjy, a source of delight for him.

To imagine living this way forever was all too seductive. The house felt right with Malcolm in it once more.

But as night fell, both of them were all too cognizant that he must go home.

That his home was not here.

Finally dinner was over, and the little girls left with their mother. Malcolm tried to say goodbye, but Benjy clung to him, his normally sunny nature turned plaintive and fussy.

As experienced parents, they both understood that with the onset of darkness, his mother's absence couldn't be ignored.

"I'm sure Vanessa's expecting you." Cleo attempted to keep any trace of bitterness from her tone.

A muscle in his jaw flexed. "I don't want to leave him this way." He faced her. "Or you."

A whole world lay within those words.

But his situation hadn't changed.

Malcolm sighed. "I'll give him a bath and help you put him to bed." He left her and ascended the staircase.

Cleo dug nails into the arms crossed over her waist.

When bedtime came, however, Benjy insisted on having both of them present, bookends bracketing the child they were desperate to protect. First Malcolm read a story, then Cleo. Malcolm lifted fat Tyrone to the covers, where he circled three times, then settled against Benjy's ribs. Benjy curled his body around the dog.

"Nana, I wish my mom was here." His little voice quavered.

Cleo pressed her lips together and met Malcolm's anguished gaze. "She will be, sweetie. And she'll be so happy to see you. I bet she'll hug you and kiss you until you can hardly stand it."

The brown eyes he'd inherited from Malcolm searched hers from a tiny, beloved face. "I won't mind." Then Benjy yawned. "Gramps, you could spend the night with us. I'll scoot over so you can share with me."

Malcolm swallowed hard. "I'm too big, sport, but you just close your eyes now, and tomorrow we'll have more fun."

"Would you hold my hand, Gramps? You, too, Nana."

Silence settled around them in the cozy darkness, each of them clasping a little boy's hand, connected by the past and an uncertain future. Kneeling on opposite sides of the same bed in the same room where another precious child's loss had ripped them apart.

An odd sort of peace descended, and Cleo, heart weary from the battleground of longing and guilt and memory, thought she could lay her head down and sleep for a month.

Benjy's hand went slack in hers, but still she held on, drifting on the tide of respite until she felt something brush her hair. A beloved voice in her ear, "Hang on, Snow."

Strong arms lifted her. Cradled her close.

Her nostrils inhaled the scent that meant safety and home. Love and hope.

Then she was settled on soft cushions, her shoes removed. Covered against the chill creeping in where firm flesh had warmed her. "Come to bed, Malcolm," she murmured as she sank deeper and deeper into dreams. "I can't sleep without you."

A kiss pressed to her brow. A pause.

Lips she'd loved for a lifetime touching her own so gently, lingering, lingering…

Then gone.

She stirred. Protested. Tried to wake.

"Shh…easy. Sleep now, sweetheart."

Stroking again, soft brushes against her hair.

Lost in the pleasure, Cleo let dreams take her.

MALCOLM STOOD over Cleo's bed and fought himself.

How easy it would be to yield. To lie down beside her, take her in his arms. He wouldn't even consider how badly he wanted to make love to her.

But it would almost be enough simply to hold her, to find his way back home.

Lose himself in her embrace.

Cleo stirred. *I can't sleep without you.* So fragile she appeared, his Snow White, pale skin and black hair, emerald-green eyes.

Once she had loved him with every breath. He had loved her the same.

Even now, the need for her was enough to bring him to his knees.

But she was as much Scarlett O'Hara, tough and principled, sturdier than she appeared. She very well might welcome him in her bed—tonight. When tomorrow dawned, however incredible the hours between—and they would be, he damn well knew that—she would be ashamed of them both for yielding.

So for the sake of a heart he treasured more than his own, Malcolm made his way out into the night alone.

CHAPTER SEVENTEEN

MALCOLM DROVE toward the condo blindly, making call after call about Ria over his cell phone headset to keep from whipping the car around and going back. If he'd ever done anything harder than leaving Cleo the first time, it was walking away now.

How many times had he lifted that delicate body and carried her off to the bed that had been their haven?

Even seeing that she'd rid herself of the bed he'd built for her with such love had done little to quell his yearning to return to the private world they'd so carelessly inhabited, never dreaming how easily it all could be lost.

He'd felt so complete there with them, once more at one with Cleo and a beloved child. If only—

He smacked the heel of his hand against the steering wheel.

Another child, not yet met but no less deserving of care, had to be considered.

And Malcolm the deal maker couldn't find a way to have them all.

Tired to the bone, he entered his garage, not surprised to see Vanessa's parking space still empty. Earlier in this day that seemed aeons long, before he'd raced off when Ria had gone missing, they'd compared schedules, and she'd said she'd be meeting with a group of colleagues for dinner, which would run late.

Even if he hadn't been so preoccupied with Ria's disappearance, he wouldn't have been concerned about what time Vanessa got home. She'd made it clear from the beginning that she was her own woman. It was part of what he'd liked about her, but now he saw it for what it was: he just didn't care. She'd never evoked the fierce, possessive feelings that Cleo called forth from him.

So how did he change that, now when his belly was leaden with the knowledge that for five long years, he'd harbored a seed of hope that the parting with Cleo was only temporary. That someday, somehow, they'd be back where they belonged: together. And the fact that they wouldn't, well, he had only himself to blame.

He stared out his windshield at nothing. After the roller coaster of fear and hope, yearning and despair, he was tapped out.

Better to feel nothing, if he could manage it. If

he let in the grief he knew was lurking, ready to strike, he'd howl at the moon and tear at his clothes.

So Malcolm released a long sigh and climbed from his car. He had to find some means to clear Cleo out of his heart to make room for a woman who couldn't hold a candle to her.

With dragging steps, he entered the dark condo. He flipped on the light and went to the entry table, scanned his mail, then dropped it all without opening anything.

A shower. That would relax some tense muscles and revive him before Vanessa arrived.

Not until he got to the bathroom did he notice what he should have seen before. The bathroom counter was neat and tidy. Almost empty. None of Vanessa's bottles and jars in sight.

He strode to her closet and jerked it open.

Empty, too.

Malcolm surveyed the bedroom, noting the signs he'd missed. It was as if she'd vanished.

Which, of course, she had. He raced to the kitchen, stomach clenched, heart in his throat.

And there he saw the folded sheet of her expensive cream vellum propped up against the phone, his name on the outside in her bold hand. Malcolm stood so still that he could hear his own pulse, feel the rush of blood in his veins.

Finally, with a hand that wasn't quite steady, he reached for the note.

Malcolm

   I'm sorry. You will hate me for this, but I can't figure out any other way. I know it will hurt you, but I just can't do what you want. I wish I could find an answer you could accept, but I'm a realist. I only wish you were. I tried to tell you, but you didn't listen.

   You won't want to see me again, so I'll spare you the scene. By the time you read this, it will be over.

   You're a good man, Malcolm. Don't blame yourself.

Vanessa

The fist that clenched his heart loosened just enough to release the anguish he'd thought only losing Cleo could rip from his chest.

He crumpled the sheet and fired it at the window. It flew like a rocket, thunked against the glass, then fell to the floor with barely a sound.

It made no dent…just as his child's loss would never be felt by anyone else. Maybe Vanessa would regret it, but she would seek refuge in her ambition and go on.

But Malcolm would never forget. *One more day, Vanessa. I had one more day. You promised.*

And he did blame himself. He hadn't had the words to make the world right. Just as with Ria. With David. A man should be able to do that for his family.

A man should protect the ones he loved, shield them from harm. The sense of failure sank in his gut like a stone.

And the only person who would understand was the woman he'd just left.

Cleo.

In that instant, it hit him that what had kept them apart tonight was gone. A tiny seed of hope stirred from barren soil; with shame, Malcolm quickly crushed it. Maybe there would be time to think about second chances, but tonight, he had a child to mourn. One he'd never even see. Never hold.

He was angry, so damn angry. Rage tore through him with the speed of a brushfire. He overturned a kitchen chair. Heaved the table on its side, searched for something else.

Then fury vanished; in its wake, his knees went rubbery. He gripped the counter and stared at the phone as a starving man eyes a crust of bread.

He could call Cleo. She would tell him she was sorry. She might even cry for his dead child.

Grief bent him double.

He sagged against the wall and slid to the floor, staring out into the darkness. All he could see was a grave that would never be, a child he could not bury beside its brother.

He groped for the phone on the floor and punched in some numbers.

Her voice was muzzy with sleep when she answered.

"Snow." And then he couldn't find the words. At last, he managed to say, "Please, Snow. I need you."

"MALCOLM?" Cleo sat up in her bed. "What's wrong?"

Only silence greeted her, but it was thick and pulsing with her fear. "Malcolm, are you all right?"

Finally, she heard him draw breath. "It's Vanessa. She…the baby—" He choked out the words. "The baby's gone, Snow. She didn't wait."

She closed her eyes. As much as she had ached over the thought of Malcolm having a child that wasn't hers, never in a million years would she have wished this on him.

"Tell me your address." She grabbed for a pencil and paper, then scribbled it down. "I'll be there in fifteen minutes."

She dressed quickly, dizzy from the whiplash of emotions. Last night, giving him up, her eyes too dry to cry, her heart filled with sawdust.

Then today. Ria. Benjy. Malcolm putting her to bed. Kissing her goodbye.

Knowing he was forever beyond her reach. Sleeping to evade the grief waiting to paint every hollow in her with dark despair.

For one instant the thought glimmered that they might have their second chance after all. Ruthlessly, she quashed it. There was something obscene about letting that thought into her mind right now.

But as she made ready, it lingered.

She crept down the stairs after slipping a note under Cammie's door, telling her where she'd be. As she drove toward Malcolm's condo, Cleo gripped the steering wheel. Malcolm needed her. It was all she had to hear.

God. Was she really ready to open herself up to love again? With this man she'd hurt so badly, who'd devastated her so much that she'd locked up her heart for five years?

But Sandor had been right. Malcolm was the only man she'd ever loved, and her best friend. She wouldn't think about love tonight, though. Her friend was in pain, and she would be there for him. Such was her resolve when she locked her car, headed up the steps, rapped on the door.

No answer. Cleo knocked harder.

Still nothing. An instant of terror. But no, Malcolm would never—

He was the strongest man she'd ever known, but how much more could he be expected to take?

"Malcolm?" Flat palms against the door, then clutching the knob—

It turned. Cleo rushed inside. Glanced around.

Spotted him in the darkened living room, crouched in a chair, head in his hands. Shoulders bowed.

She crossed to him. Knelt. "Malcolm, I'm here." She tendered one stroke to that thick, dark hair. "I'm so sorry. What can I do?"

"I keep—" He cleared his throat. "I keep wondering if there's some set of cosmic scales in force. *You can have Cleo or Ria or this baby, but not all of them. Don't be greedy, Channing.*"

He turned an anguished face to her. "Did I cause this to happen, Snow? Because I didn't want to let you go again?" He stared out the window. "Is that baby's death on my head, because I got caught up in how it felt to be home again and wished so hard that I could stay?"

"You take too much on yourself, Malcolm. Vanessa's mind was made up. You never had a chance to change it."

"I tried, Snow. I swear I did."

Malcolm's eyes were so open to her that she hurt just looking into them. Agony held this man whom she loved in its tight, cruel fist.

She didn't know what to do. Everything in her life had changed so lightning fast that she struggled to keep up.

But Malcolm needed her, so she forgot everything else and opened her arms.

He went into them like a lost sailor who'd finally found shore. Clasped her so tightly she could barely breathe. She buried her face in his shoulder and inhaled the scent of him, one that had wafted her into sleep tonight and thousands more, embedded at the cellular level as the only true fragrance of home.

A shiver ran through him. "Dear God. What have I done?"

"Oh, love…" The endearment slipped out, but she wouldn't call it back, even if she could.

"I blew it. I didn't see how desperate she was. I hardly talked to her after—"

"Malcolm, stop. You can't fix everything. You always believe that you should, but you're not God. And people can't always be mended." She pressed a kiss just behind his ear. "Even by you."

"I don't expect to."

"Oh, yes, you do. You've always been successful, achieved every goal you sought. You tried to cure Ria for years. You did your best to heal me when I was lost after David."

He jerked from her grasp. "This isn't about goals." He stalked to the window. Slammed a hand against the frame. The glass rattled. "Damn it, that baby deserved a chance to live, to be loved. I failed it, just as I did David and Ria."

He caught her eyes in the reflection. "And you, Snow," he said softly. "Most of all, you."

"You only left because I begged. The destruction of our marriage goes both ways, Malcolm. You would never have given up on us."

For a long time, he stared into the darkness. Then he revolved. Met her head-on. "So what now, Snow?"

"What do you mean?"

"There's no baby to stand between us. No Vanessa. What about the young pup?"

"Who?"

"Whatever the hell his name is. Dr. Java."

"Oh. Colin." She almost smiled at that. "No, he and I aren't—"

"Good."

"But—" On the brink of that second chance she thought she'd longed for, fear grabbed her by the throat.

"But what?" Drowning dark eyes waited patiently.

She twisted her fingers. Tried to breathe.

Malcolm, this was Malcolm. *At least be honest, Cleo.* She summoned her courage. "It would destroy me to let you into my heart again and lose you."

She'd rebuilt her life, piece by piece, after he'd left, but it had been more agony than she could survive a second time. Saying no would be much safer. Her house, her life, were already crowded with too many people's demands.

But he was the loom upon which so much of the fabric that was Cleo Channing had been woven.

"What are you saying?" His eyes widened. "Wait. You're afraid of *me?*" He closed the gap between them, disbelief and hurt giving way to temper. "You think *I'm* not scared? It damn near killed me when you sent me away." He seized her shoulders. "Goddamn you, Cleo. You had no right to hide from me. *Me.* Twenty-eight years of giving you every last corner of my soul, and you tossed it all like so much trash. How could you?" He shook her once—Malcolm, who'd never lifted even a finger to her in anger.

He dropped his hands as though he'd touched hot coals. "My God." As fast as possible, he put distance between them.

In that instant, Cleo's inner vision cleared like mist before sun, and what she learned about herself staggered her.

He was right. He'd opened himself freely to her and to their children from day one, while she'd always kept a part of herself in reserve. A small but essential fragment remained inviolate so that she would be able to rebuild when, as she'd always expected, she was alone again. The child who'd been the adult in the relationship with her mother, the girl who'd had no father to lean on, no other family of any kind, had absorbed as her earliest lesson that she was essentially on her own.

And in protecting herself from the inevitable future, she'd made it happen. Ria's rebellion… David's death…both had served, in her mind, as signposts of the coming end.

Her sensitive, intuitive elder daughter had perceived that Cleo had more to give and refused to do so. What more painful lesson could a child learn? She'd said over and over in hundreds of ways: *I need more.*

And who understood better than Cleo what it was to crave that most primal blessing, a mother's unconditional love, and be denied it?

Cleo sank heavily to the sofa. She had set out to be her mother's opposite, but in withholding her deepest self, she'd created exactly the reality she'd feared.

And nothing would ever change until she did.

"Snow, talk to me. You're as pale as milk. What's the matter?" Malcolm crouched beside her and gently took her hands.

Memories whirled around her until she was dizzy. A cold San Francisco afternoon, and a drawling stranger with a crooked grin calling her miss, while inside, she was shivering, knowing somehow that everything was about to change.

The man that stranger had become grazed the corner of her mouth with only one finger. Every neuron of her recognized his touch.

"I'm frightened, Malcolm," she whispered.

"Me, too." He drew her to her feet and clasped one of her hands against his chest, over his heart. The beat was racing, just as hers was. "But you're not alone now. Talk to me, Snow."

She tried to explain what she'd only now understood. "It hurt so much when you left. But I was… relieved. I could protect myself against everyone but you. You kept pushing me to leave the only place I'd found to hide."

Tenderly he cupped her cheek, his clasp still tight on the hand over his heart. "We wounded each other until I feared we'd bleed to death. It was like crawling through the Sahara without water to walk away from you, but I couldn't figure out what else to do. You didn't want me near. You wouldn't let me help. There was nothing left of what we'd had, as though we'd buried our whole life together with David. All the good things, all those years…"

"I couldn't deal with your pain and my own, too. I felt yours too much. And I knew—" she swallowed hard "—you blamed me. For not loving her enough."

Malcolm's eyes widened. "No. I said that, but I was wrong. I could never figure out how to make her okay, to heal whatever was tearing her apart and causing her to act as she did. I searched for a way to put things right again, but that couldn't happen because David was dead. And you'd gone into a place I couldn't follow. I needed you, Snow, but you didn't want me anymore. I loved you so much, and I couldn't reach you. I harmed you every day, just by being present." His voice was barely audible. "I once promised you I'd never let you down, that night in the park when we first made love." His eyes were the saddest thing she'd ever seen. "But I did."

Her chest ached; every breath was a struggle. "We were too close, knew exactly where the other was weak. We should have drawn together, helped each other survive. Instead, I turned away. It was how I'd always managed, before you. By locking the doors and not letting anyone inside.

"That was wrong. And cruel." With her other hand, she stroked his face. "You were my heart's blood. My soul's mate." Her voice caught on the tears that were blurring his beloved face in her vision. "And even if none of that had been true, you were the best friend I ever had. I should have reached out, not closed in. I'm sorry for that, more than I can ever say."

Malcolm's eyes were tender and hot. He pressed a kiss to each of her eyelids. "Oh, love, we've lost so much time. How I've missed you."

Then his mouth covered hers, and it was as if the long years between had never happened. Within Cleo was a small click, like the single missing piece of a puzzle fitting into place. She rose to her toes and slid her arms around his neck with a broken sob, wanting to crawl inside him and never emerge.

The sweetness of her washed over Malcolm, through him, until he knew he couldn't bear to let her go again. He held her tightly, slanting his mouth over hers to go deeper, to seal the connection.

The magic was still there. Heat roared back to life, incinerating the obstacles that had come between them.

"Snow," he muttered between kisses. "Sweet mercy." He looked into wet green eyes that blazed with the same fierce yearning.

"We—I don't—Malcolm, we shouldn't be hasty—" Biting her full lower lip, she grazed her fingers over the buckle of his belt, her voice a shade beyond breathy. "I want your hands on me so badly, but I don't think—"

He sank teeth into the spot on her neck he knew would make her scream. "You think too much, Snow. I like that about you sometimes. Lots of times." He slid his tongue down her bared throat, and her back arched. "But not now."

Her knees buckled, and he swept her up in his arms. Carried her to the sofa.

In a novel, there would have been violins and star-drenched, swirling passions, but in those first, all-too-real moments, they were awkward together, all knees and elbows and noses.

And self-conscious. "Turn out the light, Malcolm."

"Not on your life."

"I'm older now. Not everything is—"

"You're the most beautiful thing I've ever seen, and I intend to pore over every last inch."

He made good on his promise, and with each second's passage, they found steadier footing. Uncovered familiar landmarks from beneath the tangled vines and brushy undergrowth of five years spent apart.

But she couldn't quite relax. Finally, she put her finger on the problem. Grabbed his hair and yanked. "How many?"

"How many wha—" He lifted his head and blinked. "Oh."

She jerked herself to sitting, drew a pillow in front of her. "Tell me now, and let's get it over with."

"Now?" He stared at her. Frowned. Sighed loudly, then untangled his limbs from hers. Settled back into the cushions, splendidly naked. Undeniably male.

A staggering array of emotions chased over his features. He scrubbed his face. Grinned. "I'd forgotten this Cleo. Only you would insist on confronting the tough stuff at a moment like this." He threw back his head and laughed. "That's my girl. Always eats her spinach before she allows herself dessert."

"Stop that." When he didn't even attempt to stem the chuckles, she grabbed the pillow and took aim. Hit him square in the face. "It's not funny."

"You got that right." He chucked the pillow to the floor and stalked her across the cushions. "But you sure as hell are." There had always been about Malcolm the air of a lean, hungry predator, never more so than now. "You gonna make me climb a fire escape and howl at the moon again, Cleopatra?"

"Stay back." Cleo fired another pillow before she scrambled to her feet.

She nearly made it.

Neatly, he captured her and twisted their bodies so that he hit the floor first. Protecting her, as always.

"Get away from me," she fumed. "I don't want you."

"Liar." His erection made it amply clear that she hadn't discouraged him one bit.

When she struggled halfheartedly in his grip, he reversed their positions. The mirth faded, and he ducked his head. "Probably fewer than you imagine, Snow. And I wish there hadn't been even one." Chagrin washed over his features. "I probably owe apologies to some nice ladies whose only fault was that they weren't you."

"Do you have any idea how I hate that women have always fallen all over themselves for you? That first day, every woman in that café envied me."

He did a double take. "No kidding?"

Cleo bared her teeth.

Malcolm leaned in and gave her a slow, sweet, bone-melting kiss. "I never paid attention, Snow. All I could see was you. Since the beginning, you've owned my heart."

She curled into him and wanted never to let go.

But they weren't through yet. "Okay." She took a breath. "My turn."

"Uh-uh." He shook his head. "You may be a masochist, but I don't want to know. Then I'd just have to leave you and go pound the daylights out of every one of them." His words were playful but his tone was not. "The very thought of you with another man—" His jaw tightened. His embrace did, too.

For a moment they simply clung, sobered by the intrusion of the world. The past.

"One more thing, Snow, then I'm done talking." In his expression, she read acute discomfort. "I'm safe, but I'll use a condom now, if you're worried." He made as if to rise.

She stopped him. "No. And I'm...all right, too. I—"

He cut off her words with a kiss, unbridled and stormy. Then he lifted his head, and his dark eyes blazed. "There's only you now. Only us." He gripped her hips with his big hands, and Cleo arched her back, surrendering herself to him as she had to no other.

And discovering anew the sheer luxury of letting go. A slow, wicked smile curved her lips.

"You make me crazy when you do that." His voice cracked.

Her own was less than steady as she cradled his face. "I love you, Malcolm. I've never stopped. This is the first day for us. A new chapter."

Braced on arms suddenly trembling as outrageous gratitude swept through him, Malcolm paused and drank in the sight of the goal that made all his others pale.

He yearned to have this woman's love back. To grow old with her, to die in her arms.

There was such wild emotion tumbling in her eyes that he found a new patience. Settled back on his heels and twined their fingers, palm to palm. The beast that roared within him, wanting completion, fell silent before his awe.

He bent to her like a celebrant, a penitent. "This is it, Cleo. I'm never going to let you go after this, so be sure."

Once more they were in the park on that first night, exchanging the vows that had truly made them one, long before the ceremony the rest of the world witnessed.

"I am," she whispered.

"Forever, Snow."

"Forever," she repeated.

Then, like a new vow, he joined them, body and soul.

Cleo gasped, and Malcolm groaned. More than bliss, there was love here. Peace and comfort no one else could provide.

Malcolm gazed down at the woman who had been the oasis he'd been seeking for five lost and lonely years. Barely able to believe they'd made their way back.

"It's still here." Cleo echoed his thoughts. "Oh, Malcolm." She pressed against him as if seeking to banish the last traces of the long years alone.

He yielded to her as she'd surrendered to him, and soon there was no other world but their two hearts, the treasured fit of flesh to flesh, and the ecstasy of at last…after so very long apart…coming home.

MALCOLM AWOKE when she rose from his side. He watched her slip on his shirt, walk to the window and stare out.

The shirt hung off one shoulder, reached to her knees. Over the white fabric, strands of ebony spilled.

She still had the best pair of legs he'd ever seen.

The need to protect flared again. She was too delicately formed to house such courage, such a big, terrified heart.

Her forehead pressed against the window, and her shoulders drooped.

He left the sofa, moved to stand behind her without saying a word. Wrapped his arms around her and rested his cheek on her hair.

"She's out there somewhere, Malcolm, scared and lonely." A world of sorrow and regret vibrated in her tone.

"I know." The image tormented him, too. "But not for long."

"She needed more than I was willing to give. How do I live with that?"

He turned her in his arms then. "You were a good mother, Cleo, and she wasn't an easy child. But you loved her and cared for her, even when she was at her worst."

"But I didn't—"

He touched a finger to her lips. "You weren't perfect. Neither was I. So we find her and try again."

"But—"

"You're relentless. I forgot that part, too." But he had plenty of practice in handling her. Distraction was sometimes the only defense. "Where's my bed?"

"What?" She blinked. Glanced at the hallway.

"That's not mine. Neither is that brass piece of fluff in our room." He dropped the smile. "Why did you throw away the bed I made for you, Snow?"

"I could never start a new life, looking at it every day."

"So you got a new one for Dr. Java to roll around in with you?" He released her then, more hurt than he cared to admit. The bed had been a gift from his heart.

"Are we having that conversation after all, Malcolm? Is that what you're after?"

"No. Yes. No." He whirled, jealousy eating him from the inside out. "What I want is the same thing as the other night—to beat the hell out of that young cub for sleeping with my woman."

"You said pup before. Get your animals straight." Her eyes sparkled, and all he could do was stare. "Want to throw a pillow or two, instead?"

"It's not funny, Cleo." He grabbed his jeans, no longer comfortable with her, naked.

Her face fell. "You're right. I'm sorry, Malcolm." She laid a restraining hand on his wrist. "Still at the house," she mumbled.

"What?" Then her words registered. He tipped her face up. "Say that again."

"I only bought the brass bed a couple of weeks before Lola showed up. Ours is safely stored."

Relief was a cool breeze, but cobwebs of misery lingered. "I don't know if I can stand it, but I have to find out. How many—" He cleared his throat. "Who have you been with?"

She waited a long time before answering, and his heart died a little more each second.

"I never took a lover, Malcolm." Defiant green eyes dared him to poke fun.

Heartfelt thanksgiving shuddered through him. "I shouldn't be this happy." He lifted her into his arms. "But damned if I'm not." He caught her mouth in a kiss and started toward the bedroom.

"Malcolm Channing, don't you even consider it."

He jolted. "What?"

She stabbed a finger toward the hall. "Not on

that woman's mattress." Her Egyptian namesake could have been no more imperious. "You have work to do first."

He stifled a groan. "Snow, I'm dying here. I have to make love to you again. Now."

"Not yet."

"Listen, I said I'm sorry about the others. Do you want names, is that it? I don't think it's smart, but—"

She stopped his words with a kiss. "Put me down, Malcolm."

"I will later, I promise, but—"

"You can't drive with me in your arms."

He stilled. Stared.

"Come home with me. Let's put our bed back together, and we'll make love until dawn if you want. And then—" She paused.

"Then what?" he asked.

"You stay. You never, ever leave me again, no matter what stupid idea I might get into my head, and—" She bit her lip, and her eyes filled with tears.

He finished for her. "We find our daughter."

She nodded. "And bring her home for good."

He did set her down then, but only so he could wrap her tightly in his arms, resting his cheek on her hair. "And once we have our daughter back, you and I, Mrs. Channing, will be getting married. Sound about right?"

"Like a dream," she whispered.

* * * * *

Watch for Ria's story, Forgiveness, *coming in September 2006 from Superromance.*

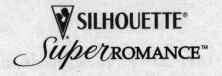

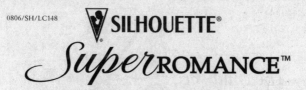

The child she loves…is his child.

And now he knows…

HER SISTER'S CHILDREN BY ROXANNE RUSTAND

When Claire Worth inherits her adorable but sad five-year-old twin nieces, their fourteen-year-old brother and a resort on Lake Superior, her life is turned upside down. Then Logan Matthews, her sister's sexy first husband turns up – will he want to break up Claire's fledgling family, when he discovers that Jason is his son?

WILD CAT AND THE MARINE BY JADE TAYLOR

One night of passion doesn't make a marriage, but it could make a child. A beautiful daughter. Cat Darnell hadn't been able to trample on her lover's dream and kept her secret. Joey was the light of her life. And now, finally, Jackson Gray was coming home…was going to meet his little girl…

On sale 4th August 2006

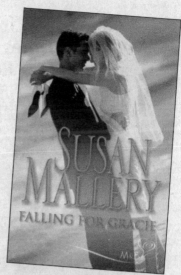

"I was fifteen when my mother finally told me the truth about my father. She didn't mean to. She meant to keep it a secret forever. If she'd succeeded it might have saved us all."

When a hauntingly familiar stranger knocks on Roberta Dutreau's door, she is compelled to begin a journey of self-discovery leading back to her childhood. But is she ready to know the truth about what happened to her, her best friend Cynthia and their mothers that tragic night ten years ago?

16th June 2006

MIRA

FREE

2 BOOKS AND A SURPRISE GIFT!

We would like to take this opportunity to thank you for reading this Silhouette® book by offering you the chance to take TWO more specially selected titles from the Superromance™ series absolutely FREE! We're also making this offer to introduce you to the benefits of the Mills & Boon® Reader Service™—

- ★ **FREE home delivery**
- ★ **FREE gifts and competitions**
- ★ **FREE monthly Newsletter**
- ★ **Books available before they're in the shops**
- ★ **Exclusive Reader Service offers**

Accepting these FREE books and gift places you under no obligation to buy; you may cancel at any time, even after receiving your free shipment. Simply complete your details below and return the entire page to the address below. You don't even need a stamp!

YES! Please send me 2 free Superromance books and a surprise gift. I understand that unless you hear from me, I will receive 4 superb new titles every month for just £3.69 each, postage and packing free. I am under no obligation to purchase any books and may cancel my subscription at any time. The free books and gift will be mine to keep in any case.

U6ZEE

Ms/Mrs/Miss/Mr...Initials ....

BLOCK CAPITALS PLEASE

Surname ....

Address ....

....

....Postcode ....

Send this whole page to:
The Reader Service, FREEPOST CN81, Croydon, CR9 3WZ